Layla

My Erotic Secret Diary

Collection 1

BSDM Erotica, Eroctic Romance, Erotica
Lesbian, Erotcia Novels - Hot Taboo Short
Sexy Stories Collection -

(4 books in 1 book)

Layla Adeline Wills

<u>Follow my on Instagram</u>

@Laila_Adeline_Wills

Table of Contents

Introduction

To those who do not know me

My name is Layla, Layla Adeline Wills. I am a 42 year old woman, I broke up with my husband a few months back and we had no children in the 6 years we were together. I now live in a rented flat in New York City, working in an important law firm as a secretary. It's not my dream job but it pays the bills.

I love writing, or I used to. It has been a very significant part of my life since I was a young girl. Well, now I want to show you my deepest darkest secret. I want to open my secret diary and tell you all my "hot" relationships and erotic adventures.

Please, do not get it twisted. I wasn't always on the wild side. I just got a push to fall off the good girl wagon.

I was a virgin until the age of 22. That's crazy, I know. Not really expected for the world we live in today but I did it. Why? I sort of believed in fairy tales. I saw myself as Sleeping Beauty. I was waiting for my "Prince" to ride in on a white horse, looking for his princess- looking for me. I was waiting for that man to come to sweep me off my feet and make me fall hopelessly in love. But I realized that the time of fairy tales already ended and I was only living in a fictitious world. I was only making a fool of myself on stupid dreams.

So things changed.

I started having fun, without looking for a serious relationship. I started going on adventures and taking the risk. I started to enjoy all the sexual experiences people my age had years back. I also started to write them down as a sort of memoir.

Now, this secret diary contains all my thoughts and emotions, some stories are scandalous and others are really spicy. Follow me on this little journey. I hope you enjoy the ride.

July 31st, 1999

I stayed up crying all night. I feel like it would be so much better if I was crying from a broken heart but that was not the case. I'm beginning to wonder if there's something wrong with me.

All my life, I made sure I placed myself in the entire right situation to get the right kind of men. The type that would love me till I'm old and grey, but here I am now, alone as always. A 22 year old fresh out of college and while my friends are having the best summer of their lives, I, as usual, am stuck at my job as a secretary for some slow-growing law firm. Where else you find a good man than in a reputable institution, right?

I've spent most of my life waiting for my 'Prince Charming' to walk through my doors and sweep me off my feet. It is becoming very obvious that that particular fantasy was not about to become a reality anytime soon. My youthful years are wasting away and I hadn't even participated in the many gifts life had to offer me. So I've decided to turn a new leaf this summer. Now I know when people say they want to turn a new leaf; they're usually referring to turning from bad to good. Mine is the reverse and it consists of a lot of planning.

Well, it begins with this diary.

"You, my dear diary, will be my dearest friend on this trip I am about to embark on. My little documentation of all my escapades." I say with a half smile.

So I've come up with the perfect plan. That's a bit exaggerated. Well, let's call it a good enough plan.

But first, some things have got to change.

In two weeks, I'm going to be attending the biggest summer party ever and it will also be my first attempt at fun since high school bonfire night. Everyone has been making a big deal out of it so I need to be prepared.

I have a short list of things to do.

-Enroll in a gym. I'm not fat or anything. Just not the societal definition of sexy. Its really nothing a few mornings at the gym can correct. Just an even tone out of my features to make them more obvious.

- Change the wardrobe. Extremely necessary.
- Develop stamina for alcohol. This might take a while of practice.
- Look hot as hell for the party
- Get laid
- Get laid
- Get laid.

I make the short not into the diary and glance into thin air.

The wait is over. Fuck love.

Let the best summer of my life begin.

August 15th, 1999

Kelsey and I had been best friends for as long as we could both remember. We were both smart and had taken all of the same classes in college, we shared similar attributes only that Kelsey was more popular enough and pretty enough to be in the cool crowd, so it shouldn't be a surprise why we were both really excited to have been invited to Dean's party. We were both 22, both fresh out of college. Dean on the other hand had been a senior from high school who had a reputation for throwing the best parties. His spring break party last year has been hyped up to be the craziest party of the year, with kegs and bottles of liquor. I had doubt that it would be the wildest party I'd ever be to - I had been to a few smaller things that friends had thrown when someone was able to get their hands on a bottle of liquor, but things never got too out of hand. We decided to meet at my house before the party to get ready together.

"What do you think about this one?" Kelsey asked as she held a top against her chest.

"Cute. How about this for me?" I replied, modeling for my friend.

Kelsey grinned. "Hmm... A little too slutty. Unless that's what you're going for, of course!"

I laughed and threw the top on the bed with the others.

"Well maybe it is! I haven't gotten any action in a while...or at all"

We laughed and picked up another outfit to critique. Standing in my bedroom in nothing but bras and panties, we were repeating a ritual we had performed hundreds of times before, nearly every time we went out to something important.

"Well if you're looking for action, it shouldn't be too hard to find some with this crowd," Kelsey said.

"These boys are just as horny and even harder to say no to than the guys our age."

I smiled. "Well then I guess we'll just have to see how the night goes, won't we?"

I wore the slutty dress. After all, most of the boys at the party had just graduated and I wouldn't have to see them anymore. So, I might as well have my fun with them. I had fooled around with a few guys before, but never had sex with any. I figured that tonight would be a good opportunity to find a cute guy, let him take me to a dark corner, and make out with him so I could finally burn off some of that sexual energy! And if things went a little further than that... well, as Kelsey said, these boys are hard to say no to, so I would have to play it by ear.

A guy happened to be pumping one of the kegs when we walked into the party, the room was dimly lit with red cups and booze littered everywhere. The DJ was doing such a great job that music coming from the speakers was enough to get you bouncing on your head.

"Let me get us some drinks" I said, heading towards the boy at the keg whose name I later found out to be Matt.

I had seen Matt around at school before, but had never talked to him. I had heard that he was a little bit of an asshole... but he was cute, so I decided to make conversation while he filled my cup. One thing led to another, and after some conversation and one or two more beers, we became overtly flirtatious with each other.

"Why don't we head upstairs, Layla?" Matt suggested as he placed his hand at the small of her back and gently guided her to the stairwell. Yes! I had told him my name. I knew exactly what he was trying to do, and decided that it was exactly what I wanted right now. I She was buzzed enough to lose my inhibitions but not too drunk to do something I would regret. As we reached the top of the stairs, I took initiative and grabbed Matt by the shirt collar, pulling him in for a deep kiss. I slid her tongue between his lips and into his mouth, finding his, instinctively moaning and relishing the feeling of having a cute guy's mouth planted on mine. It had been too long. I had waited too long for this.

Matt opened the nearest bedroom door and we rushed in, leaving the door open halfway and the lights off. As we made out, Matt worked my shirt off of me and threw it on the bed. I looked good in my jeans and bra, Kelsey had admitted the dress was a killer. As I planted a sensual kiss on Matt's neck, he gently pushed my shoulder toward the ground. He wanted me to blow him – I realized - already. We had only been making out for a couple of minutes, but Matt knew what he wanted and I figured it could be fun to indulge him. I rubbed my palm against his crotch as I knelt to the carpet and felt his hardness through the fabric of his pants. I began to breathe a little harder, having not been in this position for quite a while. I hungrily looked into Matt's eyes from my position on the floor as I unbuckled his belt and unbuttoned his pants and let them fall to his ankles. His hard cock sprung free and stared me straight in the face.

I gently wrapped one hand around the base of it and allowed my tongue to drag the underside, base to tip. As my tongue reached the tip, I locked eyes with Matt and swirled my tongue around his cockhead. He groaned with approval and rested his hand on my head, stroking my hair. I was happy that Matt was enjoying the blowjob. I had forgotten how much pleasure I got out of making guys feel good, and realizing how pleasured I was getting Matt with my mouth was getting me hornier.

I took his hard member into my mouth again, this time giving it some suction, sending all the blood to the ball head, then releasing it. Matt massaged my shoulder in response. I took a little bit more into my mouth each time went down on him. I got into rhythm, letting Matt's hard cock slide into my mouth and down my throat a bit before pulling it back out.

While I was taking a break from this rhythm, holding the dick in one hand and licking around the head, the bedroom door opened. A guy who looked my age or maybe a little less walked into the room and closed the door again. I immediately pulled my mouth off of Matt and reared back in shock, expecting Matt to yell at the boy. Instead, Matt lazily recognized that there was another person in the room before resting his hand on the back of my head and guided my soft mouth back to his cock. He wanted me to keep going! I figured it didn't make much of a difference, though I was a bit uncomfortable with the other presence in the room. But the too many drinks I had earlier taken was now taking effect, so I decided to do what Matt wanted and continued to pleasure him. I kept up my efforts on Matt, but kept an eye on the stranger in the room, too. What had he even come in to do? He should leave us already, I thought as I kept my rhythm. After a bit, I noticed that he had one palm rubbing the bulge in his pants. It was quite a large bulge! It was obvious that the stranger was getting extremely turned on by watching me work over Matt's dick. At first it weird me out, but I soon realized that my efforts had intensified as I was subconsciously to put on a good show for the stranger.

I continued to deep throat Matt, letting the tip of his cock tickle my tonsils and he in return had both hands on my shoulders, enjoying the attention. As my horniness grew, I decided to let one hand drop to my waist and unbutton my jeans, allowing one or two fingers access to my pussy allowing it to graze my pussy lips. I moaned around Matt's cock as I had my first sexual contact of the night, actually my first ever. I was so worked up that my own touch almost set off an orgasm right then. As I rubbed myself, I turned an eye towards the stranger, who was extracting his penis from the fly of his jeans. This really wasn't happening, it can't be real, l thought. My thoughts were beginning to get in the way. I had come to this party to lose my virginity but this was way too good. It was something I could only fantasize.

He was Huge! If a cock had not been in my mouth, I would have gasped at the size of this strange boy's member. It was certainly larger than any dick I had ever seen.   The stranger began to let his hand graze up and down his shaft as he watched me rub on the other dick in the room.

Matt's hips began to slowly hump in and out, thrusting his dick in and out of my mouth. I could tell that he was getting very close to orgasm, so I doubled my efforts, rubbing my tongue and lips over the sensitive tip of Mark's cock as he groaned and let loose a thick rope of his hot semen. His cum filled my mouth as I continued to pleasure him, as each string of rope came bouncing off of the walls of my mouth. I swallowed everything in a large gulp. Matt's cock stopped pulsing after a bit, and I released his softening member from my warm mouth with a pop. I opened my mouth to show him I had swallowed everything I had received from him, just as the girls in the porn movies I had watched. Matt stroked the side of my head in appreciation, and then smiling he lifted his pants and zipped them back up.

I sat on the floor, the taste of Matt's cum dominating my mouth as the other boy in the room began to advance toward me. For a moment, we had forgotten about him, I had been more concerned with making Matt nut hard that I forgot the stranger in the room. He must be another senior though I had never seen him before.   His large cock stuck out straight in front of him, and he let his hand fall to the back of my head, pulling it towards himself and guiding it to his dick. I gasped at his forwardness, assuming that I would want to suck his cock…such guts! But the closer my mouth got to him, the more I desired to taste him. I must be so good at this blowjob thing, I was determined. It would be a shame to not use my new found talent on such an interesting and large cock. I extended my tongue and wrapped it around the boy's pulsing meat.

"Good girl," he whispered as Matt acknowledged the other boy with a nod on his way out the door. Apparently, Matt was ready to get back to the party and beer. I didn't want him to go, I had more sexual hunger than just giving blowjobs he and the other boy had to satisfy.

"Get me a drink," I said. I wanted him back in the room and quick.

Matt nodded again, closing the door on his way out and I focused on the new guy. I immediately started deep throating the new guy. His cock was longer and thicker than Matt's and I was still able to get most of it down my throat, although I struggled to breathe when it was all the way in. I gave him plenty of suction when he had only his head in my mouth. I wanted to give the best blowjob possible.

After a few minutes, the door opened again. It was Matt, I could see he had a couple of beers in his hands as I looked up but continued to work the dick in my mouth. It was now covered in saliva. Matt had come back, for more. Did he really want to fuck me? I wasn't sure if I could go that far but I wanted it. My body wanted it. I wanted to be stretched beyond my limits. This would be interesting.

Matt watched me blow the other guy, admiring the talents I had recently used on him. Then he kneeled behind me and planted kisses on my neck as I sucked the cock in front of me. I moaned onto it. Matt unclasped my bra and let it fall in front of me, then allowed his hands to gently rub my breasts and nipples. I was beginning to get very horny, having a dick in my mouth and second guy massaging my tits. From behind me, Matt unbuttoned my jeans and began to slide them down to my knees. There was no resistance as they came all the way to my ankle and off of me. Matt smiled when he realized I had worn no panties.

The guy in front of me was holding my head steady and gently thrusting his large member in and out of me, fucking my mouth. Matt was kissing my naked back, along my spine and all the way down to my ass. In a swift motion, he plunged his tongue into my pussy. I continued to moan around the cock as I was being eaten out. Fuck it, I thought, Matt can do whatever he wants to me. I raised my ass off of my heels to give his mouth better access to my dripping pussy, I was getting so horny.

Matt stopped his assault on my pussy for a moment. Why had he stopped? I didn't want him to stop. If my mouth wasn't so busy, I would have turned around to find out. Then he was back again, but this time it wasn't his tongue slowly gliding into her. It took a moment for me to realize it was his dick now inside me. My heart skipped a beat as I felt the crown of his cock press against me. He had paused to hurriedly get his jeans off. He must have been hard from eating me out, and so far I was game to everything he had tried with me. He really wanted to fuck me now.

"Dear Lord," I gasped as he went even deeper into my fast becoming pool of pussy juice. I was so horny and wet. My ass was still lifted off the ground as I sucked on the guy in front of me, so Matt was able to lean forward and adjust his hips to get his cock into my wet slit. I could not resist a part of me- actually every part of me- wanted this very badly. He grabbed my hips and let it slip in even further, the little further, until he was entirely sheathed within me. My lower body shivered as I relished the feeling of his cock within me. I pressed my ass back towards his crotch, craving every inch of him inside me at that moment.

He began to pump his hips as he started to fuck me. This was great, I was so tight and I could feel my walls gripping him as he withdrew his length from me and my lips clinging to him as he let his cock slide from my slit. Then he'd push back into me, pushing harder that the former thrust and burying himself deep in me. I watched his cock continue to disappear and reappear as he fucked me, I had never imagined that I would have a cock stuffed deep in my throat and pussy tonight. Most girls wouldn't let things get this far with two complete strangers on the first night. But I wanted it and I was having it good.

I still had the other boy's cock in my mouth when the door flung open again, two of Mark's buddies walked in with their beers, then shut the door behind them. I would have said something but what could I say? I had two cocks deep inside me at the moment and was in no position to stop a couple of guys from watching. I was honestly enjoying putting on a show. I liked how I was making them horny and want me- and right now four guys were captivated by me, all of their attention on me alone.

The stranger pulled his cock from my mouth as Mark continued to fuck me like a jackhammer. He grabbed my face, aimed his large cock at my left cheek as he allowed himself to orgasm. I felt his pearly cum splash on my cheek and forehead as he came on me. He continued to jack off until his cock stopped pulsing and he was spent. I wiped the excess cum of my face with a finger, inserting the load into my mouth; he even tasted better than Matt. It felt kind of good to be used like that, and the warmth of the cum hitting my face was even more exciting.

I closed my eyes as I focused on the pleasure Matt was giving me, an orgasm beginning to build in my loins. My mouth was hanging slightly open as I began to cum. To my surprise, I felt something forcefully enter my mouth as my orgasm overtook my body. My pussy clenched and released its juices around Matt's pumping dick as his friend Roy, shoved his cock into my mouth. I let him slide his dick into the hilt as it filled my throat and my orgasm overtook my entire body.

Matt grabbed a fistful of my hair and pulled my head upwards as he fucked me doggy style. It was then I realized that Matt had told his friends that I was up there. He probably told them some slut was giving free blowjobs. A part of me that valued my reputation wanted to stop all this, and that moment but in another way it felt good being used like this for the guys' pleasure. I felt like such a slut. I knew I was going to regret this later, but it was exactly what I craved at the moment and I was going to give the boys what they came for.

The stranger had sunken into the sofa and was enjoying the sight of the slut being slammed at both ends. I realized that Matt's other friend Rick, was near me as I took Roy's hard cock back into my mouth. Rick was completely nude, stroking his length as he took in all that was going on in front of him. He reached for my arm, guiding it to his long dick. I instinctively wrapped my hand around it, but had a hard time focusing enough to give him a proper hand job. I was a slut. I had to do my best to give pleasure to all three boys.

Matt was jack hammering his meaty shaft in and out of me at a remarkable pace. From his pace and the sound of his ragged breaths, I knew he was nearing his second orgasm of the night. Was he going to cum inside me? I wanted him to offload his cum balls deep into my uterus. He slid in and out of my slick pussy before considerately pulling out as he came, sliding his wet dick back and forth across my ass as he shot his load onto my back. When he was spent, he moved from behind me to allow Roy room to mount me. I asked Roy to lie on his back, while I stepped over his rock hard cock standing tall like the Eiffel tower. I wanted to ride him, so I sat on his member, my lips spread again to welcome him. I barely noticed as Roy's already wet dick pushed past my pussy lip and up into me, filling the void inside me. He pumped his meat in and out of me, I was sure he wanted to impress me. He continued to pump, in and out, faster and faster, until his balls finally released that torrent that had been rising in them. He thrust deep into me as his cum shot deep into my belly, I felt the warmth spread upwards into my womb.

"What did you just do?" I gasped as I felt the guy's orgasm inside me for the first time.
The feeling of his hot cum shooting into my depths as I imagined his body being overtaken by extraordinary pleasure made me shudder. If I hadn't just cum a few moments ago, I certainly would have been convulsing around his dick as he came into me. Instead, I only got hornier and craved more stimulation. Roy pulled out of me to trade places with Rick, who was only too happy to have a go at my twat. I had to stop now, I just had to stop. I just had a guy cum inside me.

But Rick wasn't having any of that, he slid into me, hammering away like the others before him. I interrupted him for a moment. I was getting sore, so I decided to get on my back on the bed. This way I could watch as he slid his dick in and out of me. Roy held up a beer he had been drinking all this while to me, pouring the last of it into my mouth. I was feeling sort of drunk now. The alcohol in her system made every pound from Rick triple. He had increased his pace significantly. He was about to cum. I knew it, I wasn't going to let him cum inside me but I still wanted him inside me, maybe a little longer, just a few more thrusts.

Not Again! I whispered underneath my breath. Rick had nut inside me. His scrunched-up look on his face was all I needed to know he was overcome with pleasure. I turned my face towards the door in time to watch Kelsey enter the room. She watched them for a minute before she stepped up:

"Okay, boys, I think she's had enough. The party's over downstairs, so you should get your clothes and leave." She looked at Rick who she had already known for most of her life. He was naked, and she took some time to admire him, and noticed his sweaty chest and brow, and his limp but engorged red cock. "Looks like you had a good time…"

Rick had a slightly guilty look on his face, and then realized that Kelsey had a "boys will be boys" smirk on her face. As the other boys left the room, Kelsey said, "come on, Rick, help me get her to the shower". They helped me to my feet-my knees were weak and thighs sore- and across the room to the shower.

"I'm going to get Layla cleaned up now. We'll talk tomorrow." Kelsey was telling Rick to go.
"God Layla, you looked so sexy like that!" Kelsey said admiringly. We were alone now and Kelsey was washing the globs and streaks of cum off my body. I was sure she was surprised at what I had been up to all night, but also a little jealous. She liked to get fucked, too. I had just lived out one of her deepest fantasies. She looked at me again. She must have been thinking about all the boys who had just orgasmed because of me. Her best friend had just had an incredible, porno-movie level experience and she had missed completely and didn't even get to participate.

She was going to change that; we were best friends and did everything together, after all. She put one hand on my cheek and planted a tender kiss on my lips. I kissed back, and our tongues were soon entwined. She could taste the semen on my tongue and when we broke the kiss, she had some of the boys' seeds on her palm, too.

"Wash up Layla, it's late already," Kelsey advice as she shut the bathroom door behind her, "I'd be waiting in the other room."

August 16th 1999

Kesley had taken the liberty of getting us a taxi. The ride home was very quiet from the little I remember.. We slept most of the day and I woke with a horrible case of hangover. I watched her cook up some weird drink. I could tell from the color that it was absolutely horrible.

"Drink up." She said as she dropped a glass in front of me.

"Hell Nah." I protested.

"Its for your own good. It would get rid of the horrible headache I know you're having." I frowned as I drank the horrid drink.

"Have you seen my phone?" I asked and she pushed it to me.

I had 10 missed call from my Cousin Calvin. He was in California. We hadn't seen in a long while. He went to California to school and he never came back. He left a voice mail. He wanted me to come to California the following weekend. According to him, something fun packed was involved. I was about to refuse but Kesley talked me into it. It would be more adventures for me was her reason. In a way she was right but I really had to sleep on it though.

August 25th, 1999

It's my third day in California. The sexual tension between Calvin and I just keeps building. Last night after writing down the not too exciting details of my day, I found myself masturbating to sleep with the thought of him.

How did he get so sexy in two years? I just can't stop thinking of him wrapping those thick biceps around me. I want - scrap that, I need him to fill me up. I know it's bad to want my cousin in this way but I want it still. His baritone voice, the gentle touch, the way his muscles tighten when he surfs. I want this man so bad it's driving me crazy. Why did he have to be my cousin? I need something steamy to happen in my life this next few days.

Calvin got to the beach and met me laying out on the sand on my beach towel. I lay with my elbows propped out enjoying the morning sun and the morning waves as well. California is so beautiful. My hair was packed up in a bun, even though I was sure my surfing lessons was going to wash it all out. He planted two surfing boards, upright, in the sand when he got to me. When he said hello, my heart almost melted. He was dressed in a tank top and shorts. I, on the other hand, had on a bright red 2 piece bikini suit but I had a very large shirt covering it all. I'm still a tad bit conscious of my body even though it's gotten so much better to look at this last few weeks.

He sat next to me and we talked about school and future plans. He finally convinced me to take off my big shirt and show off my 'amazing body' as he called it. I tried to refuse but then he struck me a deal I couldn't decline. He would take off his if I take off mine. Anything to stare at that chest. So after a little deliberation, I was sitting at the beach with my cousin trying hard not to stare at my breast. If I read his eyes correctly, he was probably thinking of stretching out to untie my bikini. I had carefully selected today's bikini. It accentuated my hips and lower back perfectly. What man wouldn't like to see the most attractive areas of a woman easily?

Most Californian girls looked like athletic hot surfer chicks. I couldn't compete if I tried but somehow I had caught the eyes of my cousin, who happened to be one of the hottest guys around. In a quick description, he was a tall, blonde, athletic surfer.

I could feel myself get wet from starting at him so much. He must have noticed that I was getting pretty uncomfortable because he flashed a smile at me and asked if I was enjoying the view.
"Its the best I have seen in a long while," I said truthfully. "I wouldn't trade this for the world".

We talked for a while then I got out suntan from my bag.

"Need some?"

"Sure, thanks." He took it from my hands and took a bit.

As we worked the lotion onto our skins, I occasionally caught him taking glances at me. I caught him because I was doing the same.

I turned to him and he jerked a bit. Probably scared I had caught him staring.

"Do you mind helping me with this?" I pointed to my back acting as un-sexy as I could. But I could still hear my horniness in my own voice.

I rolled my body and lay on my stomach and turned my head to the side. I undid the tie on my bikini and spread it away from my body. He stood still for a while, probably shocked.

"I'm waiting," I said out loud.

"Oh sorry. I got distracted by something happening on the beach."

I stifled a giggle cause he wasn't in any way looking towards the beach. His eyes were fixed on me.

He lowered himself to my side and poured put a generous amount of the lotion into his palm and rubbed it to warm it up. His hands were shaking when he began to apply it on my back.

I was really happy I wasn't the only nervous one.

My heart was fluttering when he touched my skin. His hands were so strong yet so gentle. He was kneading my flesh ever so nicely I was scared I would cum from just a message.

"That feels so good." I cooed softly. I wished I could roll over so he could work his magic on my breasts as well. But that would be very inappropriate. Instead, I undid the tie on my bottoms too. He massaged the lotion into my hips and lower back. I wasn't sure if to be bothered that my cousin had his hands all over my body. From the sounds I was making, he was aware I was enjoying it.

That gave him more courage, so he moved further down. His hands led down to the back of my thighs, he spent a great deal of time working on my calves. I wished he would just remove the little fabric acting as an obstruction.

When he was done I thanked him.

"No, thank you." He said shyly.

We remained on the towel for a while before he finally helped me to tie up my bikini and bottoms.

"Time to surf." He said much to my dismay.

He gave me some verbal instructions on what to do but most of it didn't stick. I was too busy staring at his tight biceps.

"Nevermind. Just watch me." He said frustrated by my lack of attention.

He grabbed one of the boards and tucked it under his arm. He was fast on his feet as he headed for the water. When he was far enough, he placed the board underneath him and in one swift motion, he was gliding smoothly on the surface of the water. It was so awesome the way he moved. He finally turned to face the beach waiting for the perfect wave that could hit at any moment. The water came rolling in and Calvin stood as the wave caught the board lulling him forward. I screamed. It was the coolest thing I had seen in my entire life.

I wasn't with my camera it was one of those moments worth not forgetting.

He looked perfect riding that wave. The Sun and the ocean as a background.

"What would it be like riding him with the sun and ocean as a background?" I thought to myself. He looked sexy. He did some tricks on the water before coasting in and stopping a few feet from me. The water climbed to him like a second skin.

"Now your turn."

"Hell no. I could never do that?"

"You're just scared." He pulled me close. "Don't be, I got you." He said staring into my eyes.

The hours that followed were filled with me making a big fool of myself. I was never athletic or did any sports. Even if I did, surfing required an extremely different set of skills. He just kept making a joke of my disorientation. I couldn't even be mad, his laughter was so contagious and soothing to the ears. Terrible or not, I just wanted to spend time with my cousin and I was enjoying every bit of it.

After a while, I hugged him for trying to help my sorry ass. Instinctively, he wrapped his hands around my waist and pulled me close. My breasts pressed into his chest and his crotch rubbed against me. I didn't want him to let go and I think he did not want to either. We stayed like that a little longer than was appropriate before I finally let go.

"How about we take a walk?" I asked to clear the air.

He nodded then grabbed our surfboards and placed them in the sand next to my towel before leading the way.

He held my hand as we walked and it read a lot of meaning as to how we both were feeling. This whole thing was wrong but damn I was hooked.

The thought of having sex with him is most definitely not going to end well.

I know that because I stopped dead in my track and placed his palm over my left breast.

"Can you feel it?" I asked. I was done pretending. My heart was racing rapidly.

He stared at me for a while before responding.

"I've wanted you since the night you arrived." I was happy to know I wasn't the only one feeling that way.

"Me too," I replied.

"So?" He asked.

"So?"

We stared at each other for a long time.

"This is awkward." I blurted out and we both burst into laughter. When we finally calmed down he leaned towards me till our foreheads touched.

"Can we just enjoy each others company for the next couple of days?" He asked.

"I want to spend time with you. That is all I know." I responded. "I also want you badly."

I wanted to kiss him so badly but I had to refrain myself. We walked back to the beach to get our stuff and headed back to the resort. This is going to be another long night as his image is stuck in my head.

August 26th, 1999

I spent most of the day walking along the beach in my sundress and stuffing as much junk food as my stomach could carry into me. Jack was busy with a class so I couldn't disturb him. The hours till he finally walked into the bar was a blur. I was slurping on a smoothie when he walked in..

"Someone looks bored." I looked up to him. He had a weird grin on his face. I wanted to kiss it off him but I kept slurping.

"You have absolutely no idea. I've been here for almost an hour. This should be my third smoothie."

"So you came all the way from New York to pump sugar into your body." He asked with a smudge grin. I could feel myself get wet from the thought of those lips against my clit.

"Of course not. Its just extracurricular activities." I joked. He shook his head at me.

"A friend of mine is throwing a small party by the pool in the resort. Was wondering if you will be interested?"

"I'm not sure I'm dressed right for a party." I motioned to my sundress.

He took a through a look at me and swallowed hard.

"You're a little bit overdressed but it would work."

"Then I'm in." I got up from where I sat and placed the money for my drinks on the counter. "Hope all the guys won't be avoiding me because they know I'm your cousin?" It was a ploy. I just wanted to know if he told them. The only guy I was going to be all over was him and deep down he knew that.

"Never fret, for they are unaware." He said it in an accent I couldn't place.

"What accent is that?"

"Pirates." He laughed.

"Aren't you supposed to say 'arghh'." I lifted a brow.

"I'm not that type of pirate. I'm civilized."

I palmed my face at the thought of a civilized pirate. At the pool, he wasn't wrong I was overdressed. Most girls were in a 2 piece bikini. some had just one piece with dangling tits bouncing around. It reminded me of the orgy. He pulled me to a corner and I sat on his lap since there weren't many available chairs. We talked and laughed while the party went on. Often times, I would push myself into him and make sure he felt my boobs. I wished I wasn't putting on the stupid bra.

The music got really loud so I pulled him up to dance with me. I couldn't take my eyes off his lips. I wanted to kiss him so badly. And I did.

I threw my arm around his neck and pulled him close. When our lips touched, I heard fireworks.

Our tongues explored and his hand moved to my ass squeezing them firmly. I pushed my body into him, I didn't want any space between us. We were both moaning as we kissed. It took every nerve in me to pull away.

"I'm sorry I did that. " I muttered before running away to the room.

I'm not sure if he would come for me. Maybe it's not-

He's at the door. He wants to come in. I guess the night isn't over yet.

August 27th, 1999

Now last night was a blast.

He walked into the room and sat on the bed. I just started rambling about how I was sorry about kissing him and how it was probably the alcohol and I didn't mean to. I didn't even notice when he walked back to me until I was being pulled into a deep kiss. He kissed me with so much hunger and ferocity. I was short of air when he pulled away.

"I've wanted to do that since you got here." He confessed.

"This isn't right. We aren't supposed to do this."

"No one has to ever know." He pushed the hair that gel to my face to the back of my ear. He kissed me again, gently this time, supporting the nape of my neck with his hand. His had finally slid down and started to push my dress off my body. Mine was pulling his polo off his body, then his short. He slid his hand behind me an unhooked my bra. My breast came free of their cage. He nibbled at my neck kissing downwards slowly. His hands gliding down my sides and up again to fondle with my breast. They ten danced slowly down my abdomen and sat on my hip. He picked me up easily and carried me to the bed. I was now flat on my back looking up at him. He resumed kissing my lips, my neck, my breast, sucking softly on my nipples. I was going to run mad from all the soft touches.

His hands grabbed firmly on my hips before his finger hooked my panties and slid them off me.

His kisses began to go lower. They lingered over my abdomen pushing me to the edge. I would arch my back hoping he would get the message and move a little lower but he just kissed around my navel and the slight V-shape that was just forming around my abdomen.

I was trembling under him. He kissed me again, our tongues as demanding as ever. His hands finally went between my thighs and he moaned softly against my neck as I shook from the cold touch. He must have liked the fact I was smooth cause he went down on me.

He inhaled my scent sharply.

"Dear lord. You smell so good." I could be even make out a word I just kept grabbing at the sheets. I couldn't fight it when he extended his tongue and buried his head in my sex.

I gasped for air and pushed it even further closer to him. He used his tongue to play with my clit while using my hips as support and as a means to hold me down.

His other hand went up a and down my thighs and the squeezed at my butt cheek. I was dripping when he finally separated his lip from my sex.

"You taste amazing as well."

He said before placing his head back and using his tongue to penetrate as far as he could. I coiled up in surprise. His tongue motions were Swift and precise. I moved my hand to the back of his head encouraging him to go faster. I spread my legs a little bit wider to give him more access but my knees were caving in. My whole body began to shake uncontrollably against his face. He groaned against me but he never pulled away. He very stopped doing what he was doing. my scent filled the room. He pulled away when I finally stopped shaking giving me a chance to catch my breath.

I guided him up until we were face to face.

"I want you inside of me. Now." I whispered into his ear.

My body was aching for him.

I could feel his erection twitch against my leg from excitement. I tried to ignore the guilt I felt from the wrongness of it all, but I buried it away. He grabbed his short and began to search the pockets.

"What's wrong? I asked as he began to search more eagerly.

"I don't have protection." I could hear the pain in his voice.

"It's fine. Just pull out before you cum." I told him and pulled him for a kiss. "I need this inside me right now." I reached for his erection and stroked it gently.

I laid back and patted my legs. He moved closer and I could feel the tip of his penis at my vaginal entrance. He slid so slowly into me and I moaned in response. My wait was finally over. His entry was so smooth as I had juice everywhere. He pushed deeper until we were chest to chest. My walls clenched on him, tightly. He wrapped me on his arms and we remained there, closer than two people could ever be.

I kissed him again with all my raging emotions before grinding my waste against him. He began to pump slowly into my pelvis, slowly keeping a rhythm that drew soft moans from me. Gradually, he went faster. I tried to control his pace by wrapping my legs around him, but he struggled them off him as he began to drive fiercely. Even with the air conditioning, we were both sweating.

He put his hand behind my head and kissed me aggressively. I hung my legs up in the air in a V shape, offering him all of me.

I could feel him throbbing inside me. I caged him between my legs once more. The feeling against my walls was just amazing.

"I'm cumming." He groaned. Weirdly, I tightened my legs around him. I didn't want it to end. He pulled out with a little force. I quickly got off my back and grabbed his penis and began to stroke it fast. I could feel him about to burst. I placed my breast high enough to collect it. He spilled it on me, some of it got to my face but I didn't mind.

I fucked my cousin. He grabbed a towel and cleaned us both up before we got into the sheets and cuddled till we fell asleep.

March 12th, 1999

Kesley finally talked me into taking the weekend to camp with her. She had come up with this master plan for a perfect girl's night in the bush. As crazy as she sounds, I agreed. I needed a little spontaneity in my life. Of course, I left all the planning to her. I wouldn't be able to help if I wanted to.

My old law firm wasn't as stressful as the one I was in now. I am handling twice as much work with triple the pay, which makes all the stress worth it. Other benefits included meeting the different intriguing clients of my boss. I occasionally flirt with some, others flirt with me. If I'm lucky I get asked out and have fun a couple of times before one of us get tired or I chicken out when it's getting a bit serious.

Today, I was handling all of my paperwork for the weekend since I was going to be out with Kesley. My fingers were hurting from typing. All I was praying for was that Kesley had planned something extremely fun packed.

I finished with the last batch of office work and headed to my room to pack. It was just a day in the forest, so I didn't need much. I arranged my khaki shorts and a simple chiffon blouse to wear hiking. In my bag, I packed a change of clothes and undies as well as tent materials I got from a few years back and my a sleeping bag.

I was putting the last set of items into my bag when my phone rang. I picked it to see Kesley's evil grin staring back at me.

"hi!" she screeched with glee.

"hi," I said back.

"that is most definitely not excitement I hear in your voice." She sounded disappointed,

"that's because it isn't. I've been typing for hours so I can be done with my work and sleep with you in the bush tomorrow." She giggled.

"it is cute that you think I'm sexy enough for you to be with. But no, we are going to have a quiet time in the bush not orgasms." She cackled as she spoke.

"girl, you wear me out." I sighed.

"if I don't, who will." She laughed and it made me laugh too, Kesley was work but she always lifted my spirit. " so are you done the packing?"

"just finished. I packed my tent so no need to pack yours too." I explained.

"Oh I was about to tell you to pack yours, I can't remember where I kept mine. Oh and also, could you get some booze from the grocery store close to your house? We would be needing it to get all those spicy stories out of you." Now she got me laughing my guts out, she has had this notion for a while now that I had been getting more sex than she was and she wanted every little detail.

"sure, no way I would survive the jungle without lots of alcohol. Bye crazy."

"bye normal." I pulled the phone off my ear. " hold on a second!" she screamed from the other side. I dragged the phone back to my ear.

"what now?" I asked frustrated. All I needed was rest.

"just wanted you to know that I love you. Good night, see you tomorrow." She ended the call before I could reply.

What a crazy fellow, I thought to myself.

I quickly rushed out to get the drinks and came back home to my bed. Rest was very much needed.

March 13th, 1999

Kesley was knocking on my door as early as 10 am. I had just gotten out the shower. I ran to the door to open it before she pulled it down.

As usual, she spent the first 30 minutes nagging at the fact I wasn't dressed then decided to help me carry my luggage to the car while I dressed. We both had similar khaki shorts although hers was way shorter than mine. She, on the other hand, had a tank top above her short.

As soon as I was dressed, she hurriedly locked my door and pulled me out of the house. When I asked why she was so in a hurry she nagged about how we had a 2 hours drive and an hour or more walk before we got to our spot. Normally, I would have been scared but navigating a map was one of the few things I could trust Kelsey's brain with.

Loud music blared from the speaker as we drove. We used the opportunity to do a little sing-along. After about an hour, I got tired and fell asleep. Kelsey woke me up when we finally got to the park. It took a while for me to get my orientation. I got out of the car to see

Kelsey handling her map and compass. Honestly, she looked really sexy when she was being smart. I always wondered why she tried to hide this part of herself from the rest of the world. Most people didn't know she wore reading glasses or had a high. Collection of books in a hidden closet in her apartment. Her smartness was a huge turn on but she was oblivious to that. I got out our bags and stacked them together while I waited for her to finish her calculations or whatever she was doing.

"Phones off." She said as she looked up from the map and pulled out her phone from her pocket to switch it off. I did the same too, not like it was necessary. We most definitely won't be getting much connection in all that mass of trees. We grabbed our bags and started the hike. I followed as she led the way through the jungle.

We didn't talk much since she needed to concentrate on the map. She would occasionally make a small joke or just look back to make sure I was keeping up.

She was used to camping, I, on the other hand, preferred a good time indoors. When the silence became unbearable, I started to ask questions. I would ask about the name of trees and small crawling animals that would pass by us. I knew she knew them, she would give answers without a thought. I could fall for this part of Kesley and I knew a couple of guys who would too. But she kept it under lock and key. I was the only one who got to see this. She didn't even show it off at work. She made her way through the trees with ease. After about an hour she cried out, "we are here."

It was a clear land just facing the lake. I could hear the birds in the trees and the animals running. The water was very calm. The blue sky was very clear and I could see a combination of trees on the horizon.

"This is beautiful, Kay. You know you could do this as a full-time job." I said as I examined our spot.

"Guide people through trees as a full-time job?" She scoffed. "And forfeit all of my fancy parties and dresses? I will pass. I'm perfectly fine where I am."

I shook my head. There was no point trying to convince her.

We dropped our bags and began removing the tent materials. It took us another 30 minutes or more to set up the tent. Then Kesley showed me how to get wood for the fire since I was utterly bad at it. We gathered as much wood as possible and kept them in a stack beside the tent. By the time we were done setting up it was almost six. Kesley got out the extra mat she had carried along and spread it just in front of the water. She unpacked the sandwiches and waffles she had mad and I got out the beer. And we sat on the mat and ate to our full as we watched the sunset. It was finally getting dark and we listed a fire to keep warm.

"So what next?" I asked her.

"I would ask for all my heated stories now but I have a better idea." Her eyes were glowing with mischief.

"Which is?"

"Let's go skinny dipping." She said with glee.

"You must be joking. Tell me you are joking." I said in disbelief/

'"Why would I?" She asked cornily.

"Because it's late and that water should be getting cold by now." She looked at me with puppy dog eyes. "No, I'm not doing it."

She pulled closed to be and wrapped on hand around my waist.

46

"Don't be shy. Trust me this would be worth your while." She got up and started to pull down her short. She had on black lace panties that clung to her skin. She was shaven around her bikini line leaving a small patch of hair in the middle. Next was the tank top, the be underneath it matched her panties. She went ahead to unclasped her bra while kicking the sneakers off her feet. Then she turned her back to me as she slid off her panties. It made me laugh. My best friend was a crazy sexy bitch.

"I would be waiting for you in the water." She made her way slowly to the edge and I watched as inches of her body began to disappear under the water.

Her show was having an effect on me I didn't expect. She was getting me wet. When most of her body was immersed, she turned to face me. Her perky breast was hanging just above the surface of the water. Her nipples were hard. I couldn't help looking, I licked my lips.

"I'm waiting, don't be a killjoy." She giggled and tried to splash water towards me but I was way out of reach.

I got up and pulled my shirt above my head to reveal my cream colored bra. Kesley's eyes never left my skin.

She watched as I took off my flats and my shorts followed. I tried to imitate her and turned so she watched as I took off my panties. I wasn't sure if I heard clearly, but I could swear she let out a soft moan as I slid my panties off of me. I was wet but she didn't know that. The bra came off last and I walked to the lake to join her. Kesley was biting her lips as I slowly made my way into the water. I splashed some water in her face and she did the same. We got into a water fight and we were both laughing like children. The water was cool against my skin and I could feel my nipples harden. As the fight intensified Kesley disappeared into the water.

"Don't be a chicken. Come out and face me." I laughed as I screamed. It was fun being alone with her. I was about to sink in and go looking for her when I felt her hand around my waist and her lips placing soft kisses at the nape of my neck. My head was spinning. What was she doing? Her hand slid to the middle of my thighs rubbing gently.

I turned briskly to face her.

"What are you doing, Kay?" I asked with a struggled breath.

"Something I've wanted to do for a very long time." Before I could respond her lips crashed into mine hungrily. She kissed passionately. I wanted to pull away but a part of me was enjoying it. A part of me wanted it. Her hand found its way to my breast and she massaged softly her lips never separating from mine. As she kissed, she rubbed and pulled softly on my nipple. If we weren't in the water, I would probably have soaked the sheets with me.

I pulled away from her, I wasn't sure if we were supposed to be doing this.

"Kesley, we shouldn't." She just kept looking at me like she could see through my bullshit.

She moved closer and closer until we barely had space between us. I knew she was waiting for me to flinch or move but I didn't. I needed her hand on my skin again. She kissed me again, this time gently. I kissed back letting her lead. She finally pulled away, then grabbed my hand and lead me back to dry land.

"Lie on the mat. I would be right back." She headed towards the tent. My breath was labored. I couldn't believe we were about to do what we were about to so. She returned with a small purse.

"What is that? " I asked.

"Don't worry about yourself. You would find out." She crawled between my legs until we were face to face. She ground her hips into mine as we kissed with time I started to follow her pace and I could feel as our juices mixed. She pulled her lips from the line and they began to make their way down my neck. They followed a straight path to my breast and her lips swallowed my nipples. Her mouth created wet darkness against it. She tugged at the neglected nipple as she sucked. I was squirming underneath her but she didn't stop. She moved to the other breast her tongue flicking the nipple. I clenched my fist into the clothes around us. The kiss started to make its way down again. She paused just when she was directly in front of my sex. I watch as she inhaled my scent deeply like it was some sort of perfume. Her hand came in contact with my skin and I felt myself melt into the ground. She departed my labia so my clit was exposed. The cool air blew against it, her finger played with it. I could tell it was hard. She brushed against it a little more then her mouth covered it. I shook uncontrollably under her. She kept sucking and licking and occasionally using her teeth to brush against it. I could feel her retracting her head and I quickly used one of my hand to keep her there. I could hear her giggle against my hard clit in her mouth. She spread my legs farther apart and her finger found its way into my slit.

First, one then two then three. Now, her tongue was swirling around my clit and her fingers curling against my wet wall. I could feel my knees cave in. I was now screaming. My head was thrown back. I had lost every sense of control. I thrust my hips against her fingers as a scream escaped my throat. My wetness soaked the finger as I shook until my body finally came to rest. She withdrew from me and lay beside me.

I sat up and looked at her. I could tell she was raging with desire.

"My turn," I said shyly before I kissed her. Our tongues collided as I kissed. I rubbed her nipples gently but she tugged my hand to her lower body. I got her message loud and clear. I pushed two fingers into her slit. She was soaking wet. I was thrusting slowly when she broke away from our kiss.

"Touch me, Layla. Faster." I increased my pace breaking the rhythm I had earlier created. I stroked the tip of my finger over her wetness and back in. I could tell I was pushing her over the edge. It took only a few seconds and she was biting down on her lips and quivering under me. I pulled out of her and watched a smile form on the line if her face.

"Can we go one more time?" My shyness was evident in the way I spoke. She pushed me back into the ground and kissed me. She turned so she was kneeling over my head. My tongue licked her swollen lips as she made her way down my body. Her hands went around my thighs as she buried her face in my whole cunt. My hand followed her movement and soon I was face deep in her wetness. I could feel my nipples hard against her legs and her breast were pressing into my stomach. Our lips nibbled on fleshier lips and our tongues swirled on hard clits. As I came, I pushed myself into her and we ate each other it. Our faces were covered in each other's juices when we separated. We lay still from exhaustion. Kesley finally got up and helped me up as well. We rekindle the fire packed our things and went into the tent. We fell asleep cuddled in each other's arm.

March 25th 1999

It's been two weeks since Kesley and I had sex. Neither of us has said a word about it since that time. And in a way, that was good, at least for me. It was weird having sex with my cousin last year but it's by far weirder having sex with my best friend. I don't get to see my cousin every time, but Kesley id a huge part of my everyday life. We see at least twice a week. And we were seeing again this weekend, a movie date. I should not be making such a fuss about her coming over but the last time we were alone together, multiple orgasms were recorded. I keep telling myself that it was the scenery in which we found our selves but deep down I know that was not the case. I was attracted to her and I think she was attracted to me as well. And the sad part was the attraction was causing a major distraction for me at work. I've been mixing up papers and forgetting appointments, drifting in thoughts at odd moments. I needed to have a proper conversation with Kesley about the sex before I spill coffee on another new associate. I struggled to keep my head on straight at work list to avoid a query. Saturday was just two days away so I just needed to be the same for another 48 hours.

March 27th, 1999

I was filling the bowl with popcorn when I heard a knock on the door. I hurriedly cleaned my hands and ran to the door. It was 6.30 in the evening and Kay was the only guest I was expecting. But there standing beside her was Clayton. He was a reading buddy from college, who had the time had a crazy crush on me. He never got a chance to go past that stage because he wasn't my type of guy.

He had changed since I last saw him. He had a full beard now, and his hair was a bit shorter than I remembered. I was so much in shock I didn't realize I hadn't let them in or said a word.

"Aren't you going to let us in? "Kesley finally asked with her signature grin.

"Oh sorry." I stepped aside so she could walk in.

Clayton stopped in front of me and smiled.

"It's been a really long time. Hope you don't mind me just showing up here? Kay invited me." I wanted to scream at the top of my voice that I minded. I finally mustered the spirit to have the talk with Kay and now we had company.

"Not at all, it's really cool. Nice seeing you." I hugged him and let him pass by as I locked the door behind me.

This was going to be a long night, I thought to myself.

I got out the drinks from the fridge and place them on the table with the popcorn. I tried to get Kesley to follow me to the kitchen to ask why she brought Clayton with her but she just ignored me. I finally gave up and took a seat beside her directly opposite the screen. Clayton did the honors of turning off the lights and putting in the movie. I had no idea what we were watching. Lesley was in charge of the movie and I handled everything else. I'm pretty sure Clayton didn't know what we were watching either cause he had the same look of shock that I had on my face on his after the first 15 minutes if the movie. On my screen was a young lady being sucked out by a guy. My mind quickly drifted to me and Kelsey's night. She was smirking at the screen obviously I bothered by what she was seeing. She sipped on her drink and grabbed another hand full of popcorn. Clayton wriggled in chair obviously trying to hide an erection that was obviously building up. I gave Kesley a glaring stare and she just giggled at our discomfort. As the movie progressed I could feel my panties get soaked. Clayton kept tossing and turning in his chair. I wouldn't say I hated the effect the movie had on me but I didn't like it either. Yet, I couldn't take my eyes off the screen. I was hooked to every scene. I didn't even notice when Kay for up until she was sitting beside me.

She carefully used her hand to pull my dress up and rubbed against my crotch through my panties. I looked in her eyes as a moan escaped my mouth. Her mouth covered mine before another moan could escape. They were no resisting. I kissed back as passionately as it was being given. My hand slid up her body to her breast I fondled them gently through her shirt. I realized Clayton was still in the room and I looked towards him. His attention was no longer on the screen but on us. His pants weren't doing a good job of hiding his bulge. Kay motioned for him to join us and he pulled closer and sat at my other side. I was now being sandwiched by both of them. Kay pushed my hair back and started kissing along my neckline. Clayton did the same at the other side while fondling my breast with one of his hand. In between them, I massaged Clayton's throbbing cock through his pants and Kay's breast through her blouse.

Clayton kiss began to move down my body. I wasn't having a bra on so he found my nipple easily and sucked them through the fabric.

Kay left us on the couch for a bit and returned stripped to her bra and panties. As usual, it was lace, her nipples were fighting to escape the cage. She helped me pull my dress over my head while Clayton stood up to undress.

Kay took off my panties as well. Now all three of us sat on the couch and I was the only one stark naked. I licked my lips as I enjoyed the stares both of them were giving me. Both their heads landed on both of my nipples at the same time.

Kay's hand pushed my labia and worked on my clit while Clayton penetrated me with his fingers. My hand manages to pass through both their undies. Simultaneously, I stroked Clayton's hard cock while I massaged Kay's clit that was hard underneath my hand.

My hands fell from their bodies as I felt myself get close. I gripped on Clayton's thigh and sank into the chair as my orgasm hit me. It took me a fe2 minutes to get myself again and I smoothly dipped myself between Clayton's legs. I could tell his erection was begging fo4 release. I pulled down his boxers and it sprang up without much stress. He was big and he had one of those dicks that pointed right at you. I filled mouth up with the cock. He groaned as my lips made contact. I thrust my head up and down creating suction as I went. Kay found her way under me and was sucking gently on my clit. Clayton's hand was at the back of my head guiding me gently over his hard cock. Kelsey's face was buried in my cunt and she was licking and sucking harder and faster.

I was now moaning against Clayton's cock in my mouth. Kesley was about to stop, she kept going until I was vibrating above her. Right on key, Clayton released his seed into my mouth and held my head there so I would swallow it all. I took every last bit of him, I wasn't going to have it any other way before falling back.

Kelsey got up and laughed at how wasted were before pulling us up and guiding us to the room. She pushed Clayton on the bed and help me get his cock into me. I was shocked at how fast he got hard again. As I lowered myself onto his hard shaft I could feel my walls grabbed on to him. We moaned in unison. I bounced on him. I could feel my wet lips slide up and down his cock.

Kelsey's lips found my already sensitive nipples again and she sucked on them. I used one free hand to play with her taut nipples as I bounced. She did the same to running my clit as Clayton cock made his way into me. She was pushing me to my extreme, I slid off before I had another orgasm. Clayton was rather disappointed. I hadn't moved far before he threw me back on the bed. Kelsey was already laying there so I position my crotch over her face so hers asunder mine. I buried my face in her scent as I sucked on her juice. Clayton pushed his cock into me from behind. I could feel my whole body quiver. As he pounded me, Kelsey massaged his balls.

Clayton was hitting me really hard but my lips didn't leave Kelsey' a puss. He spanked me as he pulled out of me. Kay and I positioned our selves in front of him. I took his shaft in my mouth and Kay went down and sucked on his balls. He guided both our heads holding us still when we licked at a spot that drove him crazy.

Clayton finally had enough and Pulled Kelsey up by her hair and threw her on the bed. Before she could protest, he slid his thick shaft into her. She cried out as his thick shaft thrust into her, and she felt her body race close to the edge of an orgasm. She shook beneath him as he pounded hard and fast into her throbbing pussy and then, he was gone. He grabbed me and threw me on the bed just beside and fucked me just as hard as he had done her. Kelsey could still feel the hunger from her aching vagina and slid two fingers in to help her self. She was thrusting them as hard as she was using her other hand to rub her clit. As he pointed me I heard her scream out in orgasm. I came hard against Clayton's cock just by know she had just released. He wasn't about to be left out.

Clayton was out of me as fast as he had gotten in and back in her. He got her hard for a few minutes and was back to me

This continued for a few more rounds before he positioned himself above us and released all over our bodies. My thighs were shaking and my breaths were hard. Clayton fell between both of us and held us both. I was sore and couldn't get up at that moment. I let myself drift asleep. I didn't want to ruin the moment.

Twenty years later, Kelsey and I were still stuck in the same neighborhood only that this time we were both married and had started having kids of our own. At least, she was. I just wasn't ready for children yet. We would do virtually everything together from PTA meeting to soccer games and Sunday family picnics. Our families adopted our friendship and had bonded really well. I would visit her almost every morning to have coffee and talk which afforded me the convenience of watching Kelsey's son, Greg grow from a toddler to an athletic built teenager. Did I mention that I was his godmother? I would watch him during soccer games while he'd run the length of the pitch like a professional soccer player. I'd constantly crush on his tightened muscles and his defined jaw line- a testimony of long hours in the gym and on the pitch. He had a herculean build.

Greg would be turning 18 on Thanksgiving eve, and both families were making preparations to honor him by throwing him a huge birthday party just like he had always wanted. Kelsey and I were worked so hard on making his dream party a reality. Also, his team had just won the state High school soccer competition. So, it was a double celebration for us and Greg in particular. And, as his Godmother, I was committed to making this year's birthday one he wouldn't forget. But the party wasn't until the weekend.

I had always crushed on Greg, though I knew it was inappropriate. He was my god-son, meaning he was like a son to me. But Greg was so hot, his teenage herculean body was having so much effect on me, I began to get obsessed with him. I'd keep any of his stuff I could easily lay my hands on. I know that sounds creepy but what can a 42-year-old woman lusting after her best friend's son who also doubles as her godson do to ease off the heat that has long been building up inside her? I knew Kelsey would be mad if she found out but somehow I didn't care.

Greg on his path wasn't left out. I saw the way he looked at me whenever he came over to my house or when we were out on the beach or just during a soccer game. I could tell he had something brewing within him too but was too shy to let it out. I determined that I wasn't to act on my speculations or my emotions after all. Again, like I said they were inappropriate.

A few days to his birthday, I had hired Greg to help me with mowing the lawn. It would be a nice way to stuff his pocket with enough cash to get through the birthday season. A good present, isn't it? But, I kept asking myself how I was going to stand the sight of him pushing that grass cutting machine with his strong arms and with his shirt off?

Greg went into the kitchen and noticed the backdoor was open the screen door was closed. The slight movement of air through the opening smelled of earth, grass, and flowers. The musty smell dissipated quickly and he took a couple of deep breaths.

"Hello, Mrs. Jefferson" I heard Greg's voice echo from the kitchen.

"Mrs. Jefferson, are you home?" He called again.

"Greg, is that you?" I said, "come on in."

I walked through the hallway and rounded the corner into the kitchen.

"Sorry, I had to open the windows in the bedrooms to let the place breathe and clear the air," I said as I noticed him standing near the rear doorway of the kitchen. He was helping himself to a glass of water from the refrigerator. It had been a very hot day. I came up behind him and wrapped my arms around his middle giving him a hug. He crossed his arms to lay his hands on my arms and squeezed back.

"I don't think I'll ever get tired of this," I said. I noticed him sigh.

"I know, I wouldn't," he said. I released my hug and put one hand on his left shoulder to turn him. He did and our eyes met for the umpteenth time.

"what is that?" he asked curiously.

I stood on my tip toes, wrapped an arm around his neck and pulling him down to me, kissed him deeply. When we parted, we were a little breathless. He was speechless, but the look on his face said it all. What was I doing? I didn't know myself. I just felt like kissing him and I did. My hunger had started to take over.

"Um...errr...I gotta get started". He said trying to break the awkward silence that now filled the room. I could only nod my head, scared that I might say something stupid if I dared to open my mouth. He then walked through the kitchen door and into the yard.

Twenty minutes later, the grasses had been nicely mowed to an even shade of green. The scent of fresh cut grass filled the room as Greg opened the kitchen down and walked back into the kitchen, this time without a shirt. He had sweat trickling down his face, shoulders, chest, and arms. I watched him wipe his face with his shirt hanging on his shoulders.

" You're looking really sexy their stud," I said with a breathy sultry tone. He looked up and screwed his face in a grimace "if that is what I look like in your eyes while cutting grass and digging earth, then it's worth it, I guess." He said. I blew him a kiss as he walked towards me. When he got close enough, I threw my arms around his neck and hugged him tight to me. This time my hunger for his touch and his lips had totally consumed me. He tasted nice the first time and I wanted more. I placed my lips on him, this time he was more responsive, the shyness had gone away. We kissed passionately for a long moment, with our tongues ravishing each other and navigating every corner of our mouth.

I pulled away and held him at arm's length and looked him directly in the face. "you really want to do this, don't you? I said. it was more of a statement than a question. He nodded. I gave him a wry smile and started backing him up the steps towards my bedroom.

Once inside I began unbuttoning his shorts as I knelt in front of him on the floor. He looked down on me while I worked on removing his clothes. He stepped out of his shorts and boxers and took a step back. I stared at his physique and his growing shaft. In a swift movement, I cupped his dick, using my thumb to tickle the head. And then I had him in my mouth. I sucked and licked and sucked again, using my tongue to explore the length and girth of his cock and wrapping it up with a good suction around his purple cock head. He was huge, and with each lick and sucking motion in and out of my mouth, I felt his member gain more length and girth. I was preparing him for me. I wanted him inside me. I wanted my best friend's son and my god-son inside me so bad, I was dripping from my wetness.

Greg pulled me up from my kneeling position and slowly pushed me back on the bed and dropped to his knees. What did he have in mind? My mind kept wandering. What if my husband came home and found us in this position? What if someone else, maybe Kelsey was to see us like this? How'd I explained to them that I have been dying to have him inside me since I attended his first soccer game? He spread my legs apart, bringing me back to reality as he played with my nipples. When my legs were open, he leaned forward and slowly started to lick up and down my pussy. (I had no idea what to expect. I didn't know if he had ever done that before! If he had never eaten pussy before, then he was a natural!!) It felt so fucking good to have my best friend's son lick my pussy I thought I would cum right then! He took his time licking my clit and putting his tongue in my wet hole. "You taste so good Mrs. Jefferson!" he said. It felt so good I couldn't even respond with words, just moans. He reached up and put one of his fingers in my pussy and continued to lick me. He inserted another finger and started moving his hand back and forth faster and faster. I was about to cum all over my Greg's face! The thought of that pushed me over the edge and I started coming. He kept up the rhythm with his fingers and his tongue and wave after wave hit me until I finally had to push him away. He removed his fingers and licked my cum out of my pussy. I shuddered and came again on his tongue. I could hardly breathe! He let me lay there and catch my breath as he slowly moved his hand all over my body. When my breathing slowed, he leaned close and whispered, "Mrs. Jefferson, can I fuck you?" I looked him straight in the eye and said, "Please fuck me, son!"

At that, he slowly climbed on top of me. I spread my legs wanting his cock buried deep inside me. He knelt there over me and just looked at me. I could feel his cock lightly touching my pussy lips. I thrust my hips up toward him. He didn't move. I was begging for his cock in my mind and with my eyes as he looked down at me. I couldn't take it anymore, "Please! Please fuck me son!" he was like a son to me- I was his godmother. He smiled at me and lined his cock up with my wet hole and slowly pushed his cock inside me. I swear it took him five minutes to push it all the way inside of me! I was groaning and moaning, thrusting my hips up, wrapping my legs around him, all trying to get his cock deep in my pussy! I couldn't believe how much control he had! If I hadn't wanted it bad before, I was begging for it now!

He slowly started fucking me with short steady strokes. His eyes never left my face. As he picked up speed, his strokes grew longer and longer. I couldn't believe he was going to make me cum again! He never stopped as I came all over my best friend's son's cock. He fucked me straight through my orgasm! When I was done, he stopped moving and leaned down to once again take nipples in his mouth. He nibbled and tugged and licked and sucked. I felt like I was floating! Finally, he looked at me and said, "Layla, I'm going to cum inside you now." He had called me by my first name. I liked it, removing my surname and replacing it with just my first name did remove some amount of guilt off my chest. "Oh yes, Greg!" I said, "Cum inside me! I want to feel your cum inside me! I have wanted that for so long!" He moaned and I could feel his cum filling my pussy as he continued to thrust his cock deep inside me. He just kept going and going! I couldn't believe how much he had cum! I was in heaven having so much of his cum inside me! He let out a contented sigh, leaned down and kissed me and said, "I love you, Layla!" I didn't know if he meant it but I replied, "I love you too son!"

He laid down beside me and was running his fingers through my hair. It felt so go but I just couldn't help it. I just had to taste my cum and his cum together on his cock. I got on my knees and started to lick his cock and his balls. "Holy shit! Thatfeelsl so fucking good!" he said. "Mmmm!" I replied, "We taste so good together!" I sat up and gave him a long kiss so he could taste us together as well. I could feel his cock starting to grow again. I took his cock in my mouth and sucked it until it was hard again. I crawled on top of him and slid his cock into my pussy. I was sitting on my godson's cock! It was as amazing as I thought it would be! I slowly started rocking my hips back and forth enjoying the feeling. I knew it wouldn't take him long to cum in this position, so I would go for a bit and then stop. I could tell he was building up to cum. His breath quicken and I could sense frustration. I giggled. After alll, he had made me ask for it!! After he heard me giggle, he figured out what I was doing. He said, "oh ya?" and closed his eyes trying to hold back. After several times of startin and stopping, he grabbed my hips and moved me back and forth and up and down on his cock, totally lost in his own rhythm and just going with the feeling of his cock in my pussy. We both came at the same time and I collapsed on his chest. I stayed on top of Greg for a while, just enjoying the feeling. I rolled off and stood up. II didn't bother putting my dress back on, but I did pick it up.

Greg, on the other hand, got out of the bed to get himself dressed. He still looked hot as ever. I watched as he walked over to the other side of the room where he had stepped out of his clothes. He looked like a real life Greek sculpture.

"No one has to know about this, let it be our dirty little secret", I said. he smiled and nodded his head in agreement.

"Also consider this an early birthday present," I said, winking at him while I handed him my panties I had just picked up from the floor. Greg shook his head in a manner that portrayed how much he didn't want to believe what I had just said and done- what we had done. He smiled again, then walked through the door, down the stairs and out of the house.

Can't say if one or all of these events were what led me to where I am. But having sex with Greg was what ruined my marriage and also put a strain in I and Kelsey's friendship. Greg never told on me. In fact, he wanted a repeat. But my conscience caught up with me. I could no longer look Kelsey in the eye. Family dinners got awkward with Greg sitting across me and even worse when he decided to start sitting beside me. I couldn't make a scene when e would rub my lap, so I would feign appetite loss. I became distant to Collins, my husband. I would start staying late at work to avoid the conversations he wanted to have. Soon enough he assumed I was having an affair. I didn't care what he thought. Kelsey tried to intervene. But I'm sure he went to her to talk to me. To me, that was unexpected as he always felt disturbed by our relationship. He once said what he saw between us was close to the lines of lesbianism. If only he knew.

She couldn't talk to me, no one could. After a while, I got my current apartment and got out of Collins' hair. The divorce papers got to him a few weeks later. It took another one month before he realized what we might have shared was no longer salvageable. We were long lost. Or rather, u was long gone.

This was why I got my old diaries. This is why I am telling you my story. This is why there's a new story in an old book. The slut in me refused to die and it led me to my best friends son.

I can't tell her, so this secret goes with me to the grave.

I'm back to flirting again. I'm back to doing the one thing that came to me instinctively. I hope one day I have the power to forgive myself for ruining my life. But for now, I will have to be the whore I programmed myself to be at 22. Life is never going to be the same again.

I won't say I regret my actions but if I had the power to undo certain things I did I will. But I can't. So I'm going to live with it till I turn to that and return to the earth.

Love, Layla.

July 29th 2000

Kiran...that was his name. He was the Casanova type: sizing +5 inches by height, dark hair and eyes. Looking into his dark eyes would strip any girl of her conscience, especially when he smiles. He's the type that could make a girl's knee go weak in an instant. But I can also see that he's the type that would run away with whatever innocence is left in a girl's heart.

Fortunately for the two of us, I gave up on the virginity crusade a long back. After all my efforts at waiting became futile; I stopped believing in those "prince on white horses" crusade.

I met Kiran at the bookshop today. Something tells me that he came along with someone, perhaps a girlfriend or someone like that...because the thought of someone like Kiran having any interest in books is just out of logic.

The way he started to hit on me when he met me at the desk didn't give off any signs of someone who is interested in anything on the shelves.

But by God! The softness of his palms when he shook me and the smile on his face was enough to push me off my feet. He introduced himself as Kiran. And I pointed at the tag on my chest to show him my name; I ended up getting embarrassed when I realized where I was pointing to of course.

Everything about Kiran reeked of Casanova and he wore the stereotype perfectly. I can still remember his coarse voice as he introduced himself like a villain from one of those blockbuster pictures.

He told me that he works with the department of Satyation which sounded like satiation. I knew on the instant that nothing like that exists, but he looked so cute as he tucked his right hand into his pocket, pulled out a small card and gave it to me-- his cuteness made me want to play along with whatever game this is about. I reached out my right hand to collect the card from him and he made sure that his fingers grazed the back of my hand. I smiled at him and showed him the spelling "Satyation" on the card.

He looked at me, smiled and told me that they are in charge of bringing people together with their supposed Joy. In short, they are in charge of depleting people's stress.

His modus operandi made me smile; it seemed too simple and raw, but I'm not denying how good a scope it is. If the country has a package like that, then it would be a good world for girls and guys who have been pushed aside by people and their fates -- like me.

Anyways, given the chance to try out anything with this cute guy at the moment, I'd bet seven lifetimes for it! I tucked the card into my pocket and asked him what book would he like to borrow.

He gazed deeply into my eyes and told me he doesn't need another book when he has already seen one he could spend forever reading. I knew that he must've taken that hit line from somewhere other than a book, but it's effect wasn't impotent. I smiled and knew he had gotten me. Good God! Nothing is going to stop me from doing this; I'm sure calling the number on his card tonight!

July 30th 2000

Yester-night, I placed a call through to the number on the card Kiran gave me. It was one crazy call session! I was able to recognize his coarse voice right away. I told him that I'm the girl he met at the bookshop during the day, but he said he didn't meet any girl.

Though I found it awkward at first, but I knew he was trying to pull a stunt, and my haunch ended right.

He said he met an angel -- not a girl. I was forced to smile and blush as I listened to his buttering. He asked me if the day didn't end up being too long and if the night was going good.

I gave positive responses to the two questions because I wasn't ready to have things lingering, especially when I've been looking forward to where this is heading.

Then he asked why there's nobody in bed with me. I giggled and asked how he knew. He switched to his "villain's voice" mode again and told me about a well-known fact -- that angels scarcely find a partner in this hell of a world!

His words touched me deep down as the reality of what he said flashed through my mind.

Then I asked him how Satya-tion department will help me solve this, and he lifted my mood by telling me not to worry...because a befitting devil's henchman has seen me and is stuck on having me. That made me laugh again.

I like his Casanova game so much, and he cracked me up so good that I still wonder why Aunty Sheila didn't hear all my giggles and laughter.

I asked him how this devil from Satya-tion department would solve my case, and he asked me to pick between an express or stopper. I couldn't stop myself from picking the express -- curiosity always bells the cat, after all, and I wouldn't pick the stopper because stopper trains bore me out like shit!

My choice made him smile and he asked me if I can imagine what choice I've made. I told him that I want to fly free like a kite with no strings, and he commended my poetic response. Then he asked me to borrow him my right hand which I complied with. He gave me two rules: one, that I must follow his orders; two, that I must keep replying him on the phone.

I promised to do exactly as the rules stated and he asked me to place the fingers of my right hand on my forehead. I did so and told him that I have. Then he told me to start making circular motions with my fingers while I tell him all that I'm wearing.

I felt a little nervous but I pushed myself to tell him that I'm wearing only a flimsy nightgown and nothing else. He sighed deeply and I could perceive a dirty innuendo in his voice.

Then he ordered me to slide the fingers down to my cheeks and continue with the circling.

While doing so, thoughts of what Kiran could be trying to make me do started popping up in my head.

I knew he was going to make me masturbate while still on the phone, but I don't care a bit about that. I've played with my little girl a lot in the past, and it's so arousing to do it now while someone else is listening at the other end.

God! It has been quite long I had any action. In fact, I would've begged him to make me do it, if he didn't.

He made me trail my fingers down to my neck and asked me the name of my favorite actor. Kiran chuckled as I mentioned Khan.

Then he asked me to trail the fingers downwards to my bosom. I trailed as he had asked, and I kneaded for a moment. He asked me the title of my favorite book and I replied. I was so into the play as if I were his apprentice! I tried to derive all the fun I can as I squeezed my breasts harder.

Kiran's voice boomed through the phone as he asked me to trail lower till my navel. A very soft and almost silent moan escaped my lips as my fingers grazed on my ribcage on their way to my navel. I can bet the fact that he heard that moan because the phone was held right to my ears with my left hand which is starting to wish that it could join the right in its adventure. I traced circles on my belly and told Kiran what I was doing.

Then he asked me to guess the colour and size of his dick. The question took me by surprise, but the thought of what the dick inside his trunk must look like only made me crazier. I told him black and 7 inches. And he said 8.5!

It didn't matter though, because I already started sketching erotic stuffs in my head. Kiran finally asked me to go down to the garden between my legs...I was so readily obedient!

I stifled the moan that wanted to slip from my throat as my fingers made direct contact with my vagina. Perhaps, Kiran must have known.

He asked me if my garden is cleared or bushy. I couldn't help any sarcasm or humour as I blurted out that it's bushy! He chuckled wildly at my response and continued his orders. He asked me to rub my slit, then asked me to dip two fingers into it.

I was so damn wet that my fingers slipped in easily. All the while, he told me about what it would look like if he buried his dick inside me, how his dick would be covered with my oil, and how I would scream for more. This made me finger my vagina harder as I ached for relief.

Kiran continued pushing me to the brink of frustration. I couldn't help it anymore as my voice began to shake.

Few moans escaped my lips, and I fingered my vagina with desperation. Full of desires and urge for relief, Kiran asked me what his name is.

WHAT IS MY NAME?

My head went blank on the instant and all I could manage to say was fuck! He grinned wickedly but I couldn't stop my hands from invading my vagina anymore. I moaned softly as I pushed my fingers as deep as they can go.

Kiran told me that I lost to him and I've to make up for it the next day. He said that he would text me the location to meet up, then he wished me a wild night and dropped the call.

Fuck him!

I couldn't stop touching myself. I pulled out my fingers and started to rub directly on my clitoris till my body shook from orgasm.

Only after then was I able to calm down and recover. But, fuck Kiran again! He's one crazy guy and I'm liking that fact! I can't wait to go meet him. I know I'm playing into his hands, but I don't care about that...this life has always been a bitch after all, so why can't I be a bitch myself? Whoa! Did I just say that...lol.

Well, who knows...I could end up making him mine! Can't wait to get the hookup location this morning!

July 31th 2000

Dear diary,

I'm sorry I couldn't make an entry yesterday. It was one crazy day...like, it's the craziest "happy new month" day of my life! I couldn't do anything else but crash in bed after arriving late. You know, after I made my morning entry at 7 am yesterday; I was expecting Kiran to send me a text message, but no text message came in.

Around 10 am, I became anxious and started to think that this has ended even before it began. I wanted to call him, but that would seem too desperate. Though it took everything to hold myself together; I was about to lose my cool and call him.

Around 10:32, I was restlessly sitting on the sofa; my phone beeped and I saw a text, but it wasn't from Kiran's number. The highlight of the text had "Majnun searched and searched for Layla..."

At first, I thought it was one of those "daily story" messages. When I opened it; I discovered that it was Kiran trying to play a prank on me. The message went this way: Majnun searched and searched for Layla, because he didn't have her number. For me, I have your number, so, meet me right at the temple from across your bookshop's street. Be pure and holy!

I sprang from the bed as soon as I read the message. The theme of pure and holy wouldn't go too well with my tight jeans and top. I had taken my bath and groomed myself already, but a change of plans! I had to quickly strip and put on a Kurti. I grabbed a matching dupatta and checked myself out in the mirror almost a thousand times before concluding to step out of the house. I reached the temple and didn't have to look for Kiran: he was sitting right on the first staircase and waiting.

He rose from his seat as he spotted me and walked up to me. I smiled at him, but he didn't seem to be looking at my face. He walked around me two times, while still checking me out; then he said he can see that the sun couldn't wait to rise! I don't know if he was referring to my yellow dress or me, myself...but this man is sure good at buttering! I asked him if he's going to stand there watching the sunrise or grab it in his palms instead. He replied that he would stand there and watch me if only he had forever. I lowered my voice to its softest and told him to make use of the moment in his hands. This made him place his right palm on his chest as he said my voice could sweep away all the worries of the world. He looked into my eyes, put out his hand and said we need to pay an offering. Offering? It felt like the thing is turning out to be too holy for my boiling blood -- damn it! I was so restless that I wished he had sent the address of a hotel in the first place.

I placed my hand in his and he held onto it. His palm was so soft that it reminded me of his handshake and made me imagine how it would feel like if he caressed my body with it.

He led me past the entrance to the temple and made me wonder what he was up to again. He led me to the stalls adjacent to the temple and ordered some snacks. As Kiran was about to collect the wrapped snacks from the seller; I asked him about the offering.

He smiled, picked one of the snacks and pointed it at me while saying that it's his offering to the goddess of beauty. I couldn't help it; I blushed deeply as I looked around and saw people staring and smiling at us.

Kiran stepped closer to me and whispered in my ears. He said my blushing face is pretty and he asked me if that was the same way I blushed while over the phone last night. Damn him! He was all out to embarrass the hell out of me. I could feel my cheeks burning with embarrassment. Like that wasn't enough, he had to catch me stealing glances at his crotch. His reference to the night before reminded me of how he described his manhood so vividly, and I just had to weigh him out. He told me not to hurry, that I'd have it sooner or later.

God! It was all too much on me! As I watched his evil grin; I felt like kicking him right between his legs.

He started to discuss with me as we ate. Watching him speak with a full mouth made him look so local, but his well-groomed black hair and dark eyes still didn't lose their dazzling touch. I asked him why Satya-tion department was given the name.

He told me that the logic behind it is simple: Satya means partner, therefore the process of providing a partner for someone is Satya-tion...and the words pronounced in quick breaths sounds like satiation. He said it's all same to same. I couldn't stop myself from laughing as I watched him explaining so seriously, as if he was lecturing me on why I should join the Indian Army School. After treating me, I mean the goddess of beauty, to snacks and getting thanked for it; Kiran told me it's time to go. I washed my hands and forced him to do the same. He wouldn't let it slip by so simply, he drank from the public tap in front of the temple and made me do the same too. Tit for tat! I began to wonder what is up next.

Kiran led me to a red car parked at the other side of the road -- opposite the stalls. Red, open headed, and sporty -- the car fitted well into the "paint the town red" stereotype. Now this is starting to look I interesting, after all, it's been quite very long since I went around the city just for the sake of doing it. My eyes caught a paperback as soon as I sat inside the car. I asked if I could pick the book and Kiran told me that everything in the car is mine. I smiled and asked if that "everything" included the driver behind the wheel, and he replied that the driver himself comes first. I opened the paperback and discovered that the book has a series of poetry logged into it. I wondered if Kiran is really into books or if the book was just placed in the car just to attract me.

The car started and Kiran zoomed off.

I buried myself into the book and Kiran must've seen no need to distract me. He turned on the radio but made sure that it wasn't too loud --not even loud at all. The soft volume of the radio blended well with the book I was reading, and it got even better each time a good song is being aired. I read and flipped each with rapt attention, though I let Kiran in each time I saw lines that touched me deeply. While doing this, I discovered that he has a good taste when it comes to poetry and his sense of judgement is just as good! I had to take back the conclusion I had before -- that he wouldn't be the type that has any interest in the books lying on a bookshop shelf. It's not like we didn't discuss the places we passed too. We talked about our favorite spots, people and spots that we know in a particular area as we pass it by, etc. We reached a crossroad and the policeman on duty waved at us to stop. Kiran brought the car to a halt and we watched as other cars zoomed off.

Suddenly, Kiran looked at me as if he just discovered something new. I was puzzled as the look in his eyes had something crazy and improper about it. Then he asked me if I had thought of how I wanted to be kissed. I looked at him more intensely and wondered what he was up to. I told him that a lot of things have run through my head ever since the time I met him till that particular moment in the car. He probably knew that my response wouldn't take the conversation anywhere good. As I was about to start narrating the wild fantasies in my head, the policeman waved at us to move on.

Kiran took the chance, he grabbed my Kurtz and used it to pull me closer to himself, then he kissed me. The book in my hands dropped into the car. Though the kiss didn't have a good mood build up, and it didn't last for more than some seconds, but it made me close my eyes. A part of me was shocked while another part of me was thrilled. I could see the policeman making his way towards us with a pissed off look.

Then I looked around and the situation dawned on me -- our car was right at the front with a long queue behind us, and it was open headed so we're seen by everyone else. I looked at Kiran again. He grinned evilly and quickly zoomed off before the policeman could reach us. I looked back at the pitiful policeman as he cursed. I would never believe that my lips got locked with someone else's right on a busy crossroad.

One of the cars --a jeep-- that was behind us caught up with us. The jeep was filled with young guys and they hailed us before zooming off their own way. The feel of Kiran's lips on mine lingered on my mouth for a long while. My cheeks were left red from embarrassment again, and Kiran didn't let the chance slip by freely. He started to ask me if that was my first kiss. Though I can bet that he knew that wasn't my first kiss, but no matter how much I try remembering, I just couldn't find any that was as spectacular as this. I touched my lips again and Kiran asked me to memorise the memory of it.

After a while, Kiran pulled the car to a stop. I looked up and discovered that we're stopping in front of a cinema. After driving all around, I didn't expect that I would end up in a cinema. But the thoughts of the things that usually happen in a cinema erased any regret that was on my mind. Kiran opened the safe beneath the steering and brought out two spectacles and a face-cap. He tucked one spectacle into my face and wore the second.

Then he wore the face-cap roughly on my head. As I alighted, he picked my dupatta from my neck and tied it around my waist. I wondered why all these preparations were needed for the cinema. But I was wrong -- completely wrong. Kiran didn't lead me to the cinema. Instead, he led me into a different door -- it was smaller and I discovered that disks are being sold inside.

Kiran walked up to the lady at the desk and greeted her. Then he asked for the irregular and the lady smiled while checking me out. The lady left the counter and led us to one corner of the shop. She knocked on the wall three times and coughed.

I looked at Kiran and wondered what the lady was up to. I almost freaked out and quickly held unto Kiran's hand when the wall creaked and opened up like a door. A guy appeared from behind the door, shook hands with Kiran, and welcomed us in. I had second thoughts about the place but Kiran assured me that he knew what he was doing.

We stepped into the wall, the lady closed it behind us and everywhere became completely dark. The guy put on a torch and used it to lead us into another room. Kiran pulled off the spectacle from my face and told me that I must not react if I end up finding any familiar person in the place. They're there for fun, just the way I'm there for fun too. As soon as the door opened, I could hear the noise of people and a girl moaning wildly.

The sound of the girl made me feel cold up my spine as she started to beg with the dirtiest words I ever heard. Kiran placed a hand on my shoulder and urged me to move ahead as he said loud enough to my hearing that this is one of the places that the EXPRESS leads to. He told me that now is the time to fly free like a kite with no strings, else the chance would not come again. That helped me to loosen my nerves a bit. I decided to flow along with Kiran, after all, I was the one who wanted to be a bitch along with life. It was more like a cinema inside too, though the place is quite smaller and the seats are cheap. When I looked around, I saw people of both sexes mingling together --though they weren't more than seven or so.

The light was dim so nobody could be recognised completely -- if at all. I could hear whispers, groans, and moans from here and there in the room. The moaning of the girl on the screen called back my attention to it. Damn! Who would ever believe that a red joint like this existed here. I wondered how Kiran had discovered this place. It was given a good alibi and well hidden too. The ambience started to get to me. Watching the girl as she purred and moaned while three guys abused her was turning me on. The fact that they all spoke Hindi wasn't helping at all either. I've watched porn about a couple of times, but I've never done so unless in a private place -- when I'm very much alone. Kiran took the chance to torture me again. He reminded me of what his dick looked like and asked me if I would moan like the girl for him. I tried squeezing my legs together to stimulate myself, but it wasn't working enough. Kiran must've noticed me squirming in my seat. He traced the fingers of his right hand over my right knee and upwards to the thigh. I tried pushing myself more towards his hand as his fingers came nearer to my crotch. I gripped hard onto my seat as my body ached for Kiran's touch.

But Kiran didn't go for the catch, instead, he only traced around the lower part of my belly. Damn him! I bet he could see the desperation inside my eyes. I begged him to touch me there. I couldn't stand it anymore, I begged him to touch me down there.

He asked me where I meant and I blurted out that my vagina. He finally brought his fingers to my crotch and rubbed directly on it. I appreciated him by moaning loudly and closing my legs to trap his hand. He rubbed on for a while and I reached out my hand to find the crotch of his pants. As soon as my palm found his crotch, I felt his dick already hard and pushing against the material.

I started to caress his hardness as the sensations of his fingers rubbing my vagina through my clothes rippled through my body. I brought my left hand to my chest and started to squeeze my breasts.

Kiran told me that he knows his hands would never do a good job like his dick. His words permeated my senses. His voice made me horny but it also distracted me. I've never been so confused! I could feel the stream running in my crotch as my wetness leaked down to my thighs.

Kiran stopped rubbing me and pulled off his hands to my disappointment. He grabbed my hand and pulled me up from my seat. I felt weak in the knees but Kiran's hands supported me. As we started to walk out of the movie-house, he told me to let us go and get this done! The guy that led us into the inner room let us out --back into the disks shop. I put the spectacles back on. Kiran greeted the lady at the desk as we walked out of the shop. It was late in the afternoon already; the evening was just starting to set in slowly.

We hit the car and quickly hopped in.

Kiran started the car and hit the road in full speed.

Unlike what I thought, Kiran drove to the end of the city. I thought that we would use a hotel or something, but it seems that Kiran has other plans. We drove towards the end of the city at full speed. Kiran almost ran into a man pushing a trolley across the road. I bet he was as desperate as I was at the moment. Perhaps, he was even more desperate! After a while, there was almost no car coming up or going down. It felt as if we've gone beyond the residential settlements. Kiran pulled up the car into one side of the road and parked under a tree.

Then he looked over at me and asked me how I wanted to get kissed.

I decided not to let it go off so easily this time around. I removed the spectacle and dropped it on the front. Then I locked my eyes with his and crossed over to sit on his laps without breaking the eye contact. I

placed my hands around Kiran's neck and he welcomed me by placing his hands on my hips while I sat on his laps. I could feel his dick starting to harden under the pressure of my soft ass.

I told him that this is the way I want to be kissed this time around and brought my face closer to his.

As our lips got entangled, I heard the sounds of a car passing on the road. The fact that we're somewhere so open and far made it all feel so wild.

I giggled into Kiran's mouth as he shifted his hands from my hips to my ass while still kissing me. He started to fondle my ass as we continued the kiss. I brought one hand to his face and traced my fingers on his cheeks while he continued kneading my ass.

The kiss became deeper and more passionate as it lasted longer. He spanked my ass and the suddenness made me gasp into his mouth.

Kiran began to squeeze my ass harder. He would grope each ass-cheek in each palm. His touches send ripples through my bodies, especially when the tip of his fingers unconsciously graze around my crotch. At some point, I stopped kissing him.

I just placed my face so close to his whilst I enjoyed his touches with my eyes closed. He spanked my ass again, then he brought his left hand to my chest and started to squeeze my right breast. I leaned back a bit and brought my left hand to squeeze my free breast too. My breasts began to respond to the touches; they started to harden with pleasure. My breaths became heavier and I began to squirm and grind myself on Kiran's laps. Kiran brought his right hand to my chest and took over my body.

I placed my hands around his neck and threw back my head so my chest was jutting towards him. He took the cue and squeezed harder on my breasts. I groaned and grinded on him more. After a while of squeezing, he untied the dupatta around my waist, hanged it on beside him, and brought his hands to the bottom of my kurti. He started to push it up slowly.

What he wanted to do was obvious, and I helped him achieve it. I pulled off my kurti, threw it to the back of the car, and Kiran stared at my bra covered breasts as if he was drinking their sight.

Then he threw his hands around me and found the hook of the bra -- he undid it and the cups fell down to his stomach. I felt shy as I sat down on Kiran's laps with my breasts exposed. He looked right into my face and told me that the two moons on my chest are so perfect! I

t was awkward, but his buttery made me blush even when I was sitting chest-naked on his laps. He buried his face into my chest and sniffed as if my body was cocaine. He brought away his face from my chest, looked at me, and said that I make him so so hungry.

Having said that, he brought his face back to my chest and took one breast in his mouth. My hands were still around his neck. I threw back my head and a guttural moan escaped my lips as his teeth grazed on my nipple. He did the same thing to the other nipple and the response from me was only louder. I pressed my ass harder into his laps so his crotch would rub against mine.

He started to switch from one nipple to the other while rolling the mouth-free nipple in between his fingers each time. I threw myself backwards until my back was on the steering, but Karin didn't stop with his business. I was practically moaning and squirming helplessly on his laps. He brought his face away from my chest once again, and he looked into my face. I could see it in his eyes, he was as desperate as I was too. He asked me to lift my ass and I obeyed instantly. He buried his fingers into the hem of my trousers and started to pull it down.

I felt fresh air on my vagina and knew that he must've pulled down my panty along with the trouser. He asked me to do the rest of the pulling while he started to unbuckle his belt. He managed to shift around till his unzipped pants are pooled around his knees. He quickly dipped his right hand into the safe where he bought the spectacles from before and fetched out a condom. He tore the nylon and rolled the sheath on his erect manhood so easily -- as if that was what he has been doing all his life.

For a moment, I watched his throbbing dick with awe. I imagined what it would be like to impale myself on this "eight inches plus" manhood!

With my trousers pushed down around my knees, I lowered my ass to his laps, but it wasn't comfortable. Kiran noticed this and asked me to rise and pull a leg from the trouser. I planted my feet firmly on the seat beside his thighs and rose in front of his once again.

My vagina was all exposed to him and I watched him lick his lips as I pulled my right leg from the trouser. I lowered myself back on his laps and he supported me by holding onto my waist. He said he could see it in my eyes that I've never tried something like this with anyone before.

Then he told me to just bounce and ride, that the rhythm would form by itself. I looked into his eyes and nodded my head in agreement. I told him that I don't know who he is exactly, but I'm going to throw all I've got at him. I lowered myself unto him and felt the head of his dick on my vagina opening.

Though his breath became heavy, he didn't break the eye contact. He told me that he's an escort boy, that Satya-tion department is an escort agency. I heard all that he said, but what mattered at the point was the head of his manhood rubbing against the opening of my vagina. The girls he has kissed before, the breasts he has sucked, the vaginas he had sex with -- all those didn't matter, cause nothing could stop me from joining the list.

Though his revelation made me know that this would probably not work as love, but the last thing I was ever going to do was to lose flight after having become a wild kite. I lowered myself on Kiran and he held tightly onto my waist as the big tip of his manhood split and assaulted my vagina. I groaned loudly as I felt his thickness ripping me. He held me in place for a while, neither of us moved.

Then he told me to rise, and stopped me halfway. He asked me to lower myself on him again. He repeated this about three times, then he brought his face closer to mine and kissed me while I was sitting on his dick. Our lips rolled over one another and he bit my lips. It was soft and quick at first, but he did it again and I had to groan before he let go of my lips. That made us both to giggle as if we're teenagers. Kiran slid his palms underneath my ass and used that as leverage to push me upwards. I felt myself becoming empty as I slid off of his dick. Then he reduced the force exerted on my ass and I began to slide back down while his dick filled me. His entry felt better because my vagina already adapted to his size.

He didn't need to be the one lifting me again. I started lifting my ass and grinding it back on his warm rod. Kiran told me to go faster and I increased my pace. He spanked my ass again and again till I screamed out. He stopped and started to thrust upwards each time I lowered myself on him. The sounds of my ass slapping against his thighs filled the air, shortly before I started to moan from the pleasure.

Kiran's breath became heavier as he continued matching his rhythm with mine. He took each of my nipples between his fingers and pressed them. I felt the pain and grunted, but it was also pleasurable. I continued bouncing on Kiran's manhood and he continued thrusting up into me. I forgot about the place that we're in, I forgot about the risks of being caught, I started to moan wildly. All that mattered to me at that time was the pleasure from the sex; I couldn't think of anything else. I felt my legs becoming numb and weak.

I started to grind on Kiran instead of bouncing on him. He must've noticed it too. He shot his right hand to the centre of my legs and started to run on my clitoris. The pleasure bursting through my body was so much that I couldn't even grind nor move on his laps anymore. I held onto his neck tightly and moaned loudly as he continued rubbing my clitoris. I'm not too sure, but I said some extremely dirty stuffs to him while at it. Whether a car was passing or not stopped mattering even before then. My body stiffened and I felt like I would go crazy, especially because Kiran still didn't stop abusing my clitoris. It felt as if my clitoris was the only thing alive in my body...and it was purging too much pleasure than I can handle.

My head went blank as if I blacked out. The next thing I knew was that my body was buckling and Kiran was holding me to him as firmly as he could. His eyes were shut and his mouth was hanging open as he groaned. After a while, Kiran had stopped toying with my vagina...I relaxed and started to recover from the orgasm.

He looked up at me and told me I'm not as bad as I should be. I don't know what that meant, but I could feel his dick starting to get hard all over. We had sex again, this time we used the back seat and he was impaling me. It was a crazy day! Like, I can still feel it down there. I'm still sore from the sexcapade.

I know that Kiran and I will probably not last so long, I know what the work of an escort is like...but I'm ready to spend as much time as we can together.

August 5th 2000

The first Saturday of the month has always been used to set up the bookshop. Aunty Sheila and I would rearrange the books on the shelves. We use that chance to take note of any book that the shop is lacking and the ones that are rotting away on the shelves.

Today, Aunty Sheila couldn't make it because she had to go to the Akshay's. Well, it's not the first time this would be happening. And it's not like I can't handle things myself.

It got better when Kiran opted to give a helping hand. I could use some of his troublemaking on a day that I expected to be boring.

I arrived at the shop around 8 in the morning. The cleanup always lasted for the whole day and the shop would be closed from the business. I waited for a few minutes then brought out the brooms and rags, and the entry book.

At some point, I hoped that Kiran would come along with some guys -- perhaps his friends or whatever. I believed that having the shop bustling with crowd would help erase the boredom and all, though it's something I can do all on my own.

Kiran arrived around 10 am. I knew I had to throw some attitudes because I had expected him to come a bit earlier. He knocked at the door and ushered himself in. Though he was the only one I was expecting, I had to check who is it that came in. He smiled and said the morning is good. I corked my lips and told him that flowers start to wither if spring doesn't come in time.

He apologised and told me that he had to go to the department and call himself off for the day.

When I heard that, I couldn't give him attitudes anymore. I walked up to him and hugged him. He held his hands tight around my body as he pulled me closer to his chest. He told me that the sunflower should lift its mood now that the sun is up. I had to plead with him before he let go of me. He asked how the work was supposed to go and I explained how it has always been done to him. I took the chance to tell him that I expected him to come along with people, after all, I told him he's coming to work.

Kiran looked at me and told me that he brought along the whole world in his biceps. His dark eyes are still as alluring as ever, especially when he smiled. Kiran suggested that we divide the shop into territories. I concluded that the idea wasn't bad. We made our territories by dividing the shelves, and we started to work. Kiran kept humming every now and then. If he's not doing that, then he's either telling me about a book, asking me questions, or peeping at me with funny faces. By the next two hours, the work was almost done. Kiran was only two shelves away from me. I asked him if he has taken note of anything, and that started it. He told me to stay just the way I'm. I was puzzled at first, because I didn't know what could've warranted that. I was about to pick a book from the middle row of a shelf. Kiran walked up to me and I turned my neck to look at him. I saw the evil grin on his face and knew what he might be up to -- he always had that grin and look whenever he's up to something crazy.

I discovered that I'm in a really good position to be taunted --with my upper body bent, while my hands leaned on the shelf. Kiran walked up behind me and spanked my ass hard. I hissed softly as the sound echoed in the shop. He told me that it's his lucky day and I heard sounds that seemed like he was unbuckling his belt. He told me to imagine myself having sex in my Aunt's bookshop.

Damn! I've never been crazy enough to think of that. Like...right there in the bookshop!

The fact of it was turning me on. It was indeed his lucky day, because the only means of monitoring the shop has always been I or Aunt's eyes. Aunt wasn't, so I'm left to be the boss. In short, Kiran could go ahead with whatever he liked. And he did just that! He undid the button of my jean and pulled it down to my knees. He told me that my ass has been looking like a melon these days, then he spanked me and apologised that he only wanted to slap the panty.

Damn him! He knows how to come up with trouble, always. He spanked me again and I grunted from the stinging pain that his palm left on my ass. Then he pulled my panty to join my jean around my legs. He knelt down behind me and buried his face into my ass without warning.

The slippery feel of his tongue on my vagina almost made me jump. Kiran told me to relax my nerves else we would end up destroying the shop. He laughed as he said it and I also realised that about seven shelves would fall if I should carelessly push the one my hand was on. He brought back his face to my canal and started darting his tongue all around my womanhood -- in and out, and all over the lips. He used his hands to pull my ass-cheeks wide apart and told me that my anus is winking at him. I held my breath as the tip of his nose rubbed around my anus. I felt so embarrassed that I didn't have the chance to clean up especially before this. Kiran continued manipulating me. He licked his fingers and stuck two of them into my vagina, then he started to work one into my asshole.

He asked me to breathe out and relax, but my asshole was so tight that his index finger couldn't enter. He asked if there's anything we could use as a lubricant but I told him there isn't. He gave it to my asshole after telling me that today isn't the day to break me. He increased the speed of his fingers piston in and out of my vagina. I did all I could to hold back myself from moaning, but my body started to act on its own and I couldn't stop the sounds from my throat. I begged him to stick his dick into my vagina already, and he complied. I felt his thick head pushing against my entrance as he began his assault. I couldn't stop myself from gripping the shelf firmly, tilting my head, and howling softly. He started pushing in and out of my hole and I moaned with pleasure.

My vagina took over my brain and I lost grip on time and everything else. The shop's door flung open and I heard someone's greeting.

The voice was a female's.

Kiran stopped moving in and out of me at once. I was shocked at first, but Kiran rubbed my back, leaned into me, and whispered to me -- told me to reply the person as casually as I can.

Though Kiran had stopped moving, his cock has a mind of its own and didn't. I could feel him throbbing inside me, and that didn't help in any way. I coughed softly to compose myself and responded to the person without seeing her face.

She asked if we have any book about meditation and I told her that the shop is closed. She said that she saw the notice at the front of the shop, but she had no choice because ours was the only bookshop around the area. Kiran started to move and I almost lost it. I felt some inches of his dick slowly pull out from inside me, then it slid back in.

Damn him! I wasn't even done with the lady yet. I tried to stop him but that only ended in some noise.

The lady asked if I was okay and I told her that I was in the middle of arranging some books. The lady said she would come back again and exited the shop.

As soon as the lady left, Kiran picked his pace before I could make any complaint. All that poured from my mouth was nothing but groans as Kiran started hitting hard into me.

The sounds of his body clapping against mine echoed in the shop. I started to moan louder and louder till he poured his sperm inside me. The throbbing of his manhood as he ejaculated pushed me off the edge and I purred with pleasure. Kiran quickly lifted me away from the shelf as my body buckled with pleasure.

Oh God! It was one crazy sex! I can't wait for the first Saturday of next month again!

February 3st, 2001

I sat in my chair, bored out of my mind as the meeting dragged on and on. Most people had done their presentations, and most of them were uninspiring. I wasn't normally invited to present, but I'd been asked this time to participate. The presentations were about ways in which we thought we could improve the company workplace. As receptionist, they thought I might have some valid ideas. Or the boss just wanted to put me out, quite possibly. He has that kind of a reputation.

Anyway, we were more than an hour into the meeting/presentations and my turn hadn't yet come up. There had been a lot of very similar slide-shows, talking about a 'more inspiring environment', with suggestions about painting walls 'quirky' colours or introducing 'open space' offices, whatever that means. It was as though everyone forgot that we were working at a serious law firm, and had little choice but to stay old-fashioned. Trendy law firms don't get taken seriously, and we're certainly not a trendy bunch.

However, and here's the catch, the young intern – fresh out of university – was definitely trendy.

Tom, his name was. He hadn't been asked to present, which was a shame because we'd all have liked to break up the meeting by having an excuse to drool at him for several minutes. And I'm not just saying that because I had a 'thing' with him.

The chemistry was there the moment Tom first walked into the building. He'd approached my desk and placed both hands firmly on the table.

"Pleased to meet you," I'd said, politely and professionally.

"The pleasure's *all* mine," he'd said flirtatiously.

That night we'd gone out for a drink, after work. Of course, one drink led to another, and another led to, well, all kinds of things.

By the time we landed in this meeting together, two weeks had passed. We'd also developed quite a hot, casual relationship by this point. Nobody knew, except the two of us.

"Layla," my boss said, smirking at me. He thought I was stupid, he didn't try to hide it. The man's a sexist pig. I stood up and smiled back at him. I wasn't going to become fazed by his attitude.

"Thank you," I said, standing up and walking to the front of the small meeting room. There were 9 of us in there in total. "Thanks for all of your presentations," I started...

...My presentation, like the rest of them, was dull and uninspiring. I said a couple of environmental suggestions, mentioned how great it was to have young interns like Tom, reiterated a couple of the points others had made and went on to show some examples I'd found on the internet of other workplaces. It was when I got to the examples part that Tom started. I almost thought he'd forgotten.

As I clicked on my slide-show to share a picture of a law firm with huge balconies, so they could work outside in the summer, I felt a buzzing in my panties. I felt my face flushing, worried that it might be audible to the others in the room, but nobody seemed to have noticed a thing. I looked at Tom. He also managed to stay nonchalant.

I talked a little bit louder.

"As you can see," I said, my voice breaking slightly, "The workplace these lawyers are working in not only enhances productivity," I spoke a little louder as the vibrations got stronger, "But it also was proven to massively boost their client-base."

I got the statistics up on the screen. The people in the room murmured. Tom turned the vibrator up even more. I still had two more examples to show.

We got onto the next one. It was an office with things like hammocks and pool tables. I wasn't sold by it, but I presented its case.

"Having a workplace like this actually encourages people to do more work," I explained, "As they have the option of relaxing properly in their breaks, so they are less preoccupied, when tired, with thoughts of leaving the office."

More murmurs. Tom smirked at me. I raced through my final example, then on to the conclusion. The pleasure was starting to take over me. I needed to fuck Tom. I needed to fuck him NOW.

I can't even remember what I said during my conclusion as I was too busy staring at Tom. The rest of the room were too tired, by this point, to notice.

"Any questions?" I asked. He'd turned it up more and I was struggling to hide the pleasure in my face.

Tom put his hand up.

"Tom?" I asked, my voice high and breathless.

"Layla," he said, seriously, "Which is your favourite of the examples?"

I wasn't sure whether he was asking it pointlessly, or whether it was code. Did he want me to tell him something about the strength of the vibrator.

"The middle one," I said, desperately. The way he had set it now was too high. I could hardly hide the fact that I was being pleasured.

He turned it down a little, putting me in a tiny bit more control.

"Any more questions?" I asked. There seemed to be minutes of silence, but it was probably just seconds. The vibrations were at medium strength in my panties and I was soaking wet. I looked at Tom and felt intense desire. His twinkling eyes looked naughtily at me, whilst his defined cheekbones looked even manlier than normal. He wore a white shirt, and he was the only person in the room who had unbuttoned his top two buttons. I could see the top of his chest and I was staring at it. As the vibrations continued to stimulated me, I almost moaned as my eyes devoured Tom.

Luckily, the boss stood up. He was looking at me weirdly, like he knew, but I looked away from him. I felt my face burning again. I looked at Tom, who smirked at me. He turned the vibrator off, suddenly.

"No," I accidentally said aloud. Faces turned to stare at me, but I disguised it with a cough. Nobody said anything. I heard Tom laughing quietly.

"Thank you, everybody," said the boss, looking suspiciously at Tom, who also suddenly let out a pretend cough.

"Let's meet up again tomorrow, when we've had time to let everything sink in," said the boss.

Everybody was relieved to get out of the meeting room, but nobody more than me and Tom. It was the end of the day, so we could all go home. Two of us didn't need to establish that we would be leaving together.

February 14st, 2001

It was Saturday morning, after a long week at work and I was still in bed at 9.20am. I felt great in my new, silky night dress and was enjoying the time to myself. Since my husband and I split up, I've really enjoyed these morning to myself. I have books on my bedside table, vibrators in my drawer and time, time, time to spare.

On this particular morning, I chose 'Restraint' for my morning reading. It was, of course, an erotic novel, which explored BDSM in the form of a submissive woman and a dominant man.

As I read the book, I was excited by the protagonist's feelings of desire. She was willingly giving herself to this man, but one running theme throughout the story was her own, awakened lust. It reminded me of myself. The woman in the book found herself, after allowing the man to dominate her, becoming aroused by all kinds of events. She caught herself masturbating a lot more frequently, looking at people differently and just generally feeling more... alive. Like myself after I embraced my sexual side, at the grand old age of 42!

There was a scene in the book, where the woman was being seduced by the powerful man. He'd lifted her shoe over his cock, rubbing himself with it, then he licked the leather of her boot before pulling her down, to straddle him, to fuck him or to be fucked by him. Neither were sure.

I put the book down and replaced it with a vibrator.

As I rubbed the vibrator slowly across my clitoris, at a medium speed, I imagined an encounter with a stranger. In my head was a dark-haired, tall, anonymous man. He viewed me with desire and he lifted my legs, close to his face. He licked my ankles, then up to my thighs. He licked my clitoris and looked up into my eyes.

I turned up the speed of the vibrator.

The stranger had his cock out, now. He was pointing it at me meaningfully. I was grabbing for it and sticking my tongue out, playfully. He was going to fuck me, urgently and passionately. I turned the vibrator up to full speed and pushed it into my vagina. Soaked in my natural lubrication, I pulled it out of my vagina and rubbed it rapidly across my clitoris again. My heart pounded as the pleasurable sensations began to spread. I was getting close to coming, but I wanted to prolong the build-up. I wanted the release to be strong; I was in no rush, after all.

I turned the speed down a little and moaned with pleasure as it gently stimulated my clit. I imagined the stranger's cock, rubbing against me.

Knock, knock, knock.

I sat up straight, panicking. The doorbell rang immediately after the knocking. Of course, it was the postman.

I'd ordered a gift for my best friend's birthday, which was to be delivered that day. I was seeing her in the evening, so couldn't allow it to be delayed. I turned down the vibrator and rushed out of bed.

"Just a second," I called, rushing across my apartment. I'd pulled my night dress down but I was still soaking wet. My heart was racing and my hair was all over the place. I unlocked the door and opened it to the cool, chilled out looking postman.

"Parcel for Layla Wills," he said, smiling at me. The man was around 35 – younger than me – and he looked amazingly relaxed considering his run-around job.

"That's me," I said, smiling back at him. I ran my fingers through my blonde, wavy hair, then reached out to take the package. He couldn't help but look down at my bare thighs.

"Layy-la," he started singing at me, laughing. I looked at him in alarm as he continued, "You got me on my knees! Layyy-la!"

I shook my head, baffled.

"It's one of my favourite songs," he said, nodding with appreciation.

"That's cool," I said. I hadn't even heard it before. How had I got to 42 without knowing there was a song called

'Layla'? He went on, later, to tell me that it was by Eric Clapton. But many things preceded that conversation!

"You look amazingly relaxed," I said, "For a postman."

He shrugged his shoulders. "It's Saturday," he said, "I'm trying to enjoy myself!"

I nodded and laughed. He turned to walk away, when – to my own surprise as much as his – I found myself singing.

"Wait a minute, Mr Postman..." The words fell out of my mouth in a slow, almost husky way. He raised his eyebrows at me and looked again at my thighs, then my large breasts which were almost entirely on show. He fixed his gaze there for several seconds, prompting me to push them together with my arms. As I did this, he shook his head slightly and looked up at me.

"Would you like to come in?" I asked him, smiling at him flirtatiously and still pushing my breasts together. He nodded whilst staring me straight in the eye, looked around quickly, then followed me inside.

I walked, casually into the kitchen.

"Cup of tea?" I asked him. I could feel his gaze in my ass as he walked behind me. He didn't reply. I walked to the kettle, enjoying feeling his stare. I turned around to look at him. He was still smiling – he had the kind of face that seemed as though he couldn't help it. His green eyes seemed to shine like emeralds and he stared into mine confidently. He took of his jacket.

"Tea would be great," he said, putting his jacket down on the back of my kitchen chair.

I pulled out two mugs, then put them down. Before I could pick up a teabag, he was right behind me.

"But you didn't just invite me in for that, did you?" He whispered. His hand found my breast and stroked my erect nipple, then ran down my body to my thigh. He stroked the front of my thigh as I turned my head to kiss him. Our kiss was immediately hungry and passionate, and we both forgot about the tea. He touched my inner thigh, which was still glistening with my own lubrication and moaned as he felt the heat and wetness coming from my vagina. He pulled my body into his and I felt his erection poking through his trousers.

"You're so hot," he whispered as I ground my wet vagina against his cock. I reached down for his belt and undid it, pulling it out from the loops in his trousers. He took the belt from my hands and began to wrap it around his hand.

"Bend over," he instructed.

Now extremely aroused, I bent over the kitchen table. My bare ass pointed at him and he stroked it firmly. Suddenly, he spanked me. My body bucked with surprise at his first strike, but he soon hit me again. I was expecting it, that time, and squealed with pleasure. There was a pause whilst I heard him playing with his belt. I thought I knew what was going to happen next. I kicked my leg up behind me in anticipation.

After what seemed like eternity, I felt another strike against my buttock. This time, it wasn't from the post man's hand. The sensation was sharp and more intense. I liked it. I wanted more.

"Yes!" I moaned, hoping that he'd do it again. "Yes! Hit me!"

The postman struck me again, then stroked my ass with his hand. He teased the opening of my vagina with his finger and I writhed and tried to push myself into him.

"Oh, God," I moaned, "Oh, God! Please, please fuck me!"

The postman struck my ass again with the belt.

"Not yet," he said. His voice was deep and authoritative. I couldn't believe my luck. I reached around to grab his cock.

After letting me feel the hard, erect penis beneath his trousers, he moved my hand away. He unbuttoned them and pulled them down, along with his boxer shorts. He took off his shirt so that he was fully naked as I remained bent over the table.

"On your knees," he said firmly. I slid away from the table and knelt before him.

I looked up at the postman as I eagerly gripped on to his cock.

"Mmm," I said, before licking his balls. With his cock in my hand, I licked across his balls several times, watching the pleasure grow in his face. I licked up the length of his cock, then across the tip several times. He started to thrust towards my mouth, and I wanted to suck him so much, I couldn't wait any longer than he could. I took his length in my mouth and let his dick hit the back of my throat. My head moved back and forth as I sucked enthusiastically on his cock. I was so horny; I wanted to feel that cock in my soaking pussy. I kept sucking him and watching his gorgeous face distort with the pleasure he was receiving. I stroked his balls and slapped them lightly. I wanted him to fuck me. I stared into his eyes. *Fuck me* I tried to beg, wordlessly.

He seemed to respond to my plea, as he pulled his cock slowly out of my mouth.

"Get back over the table," he said.

I kissed his cock again as he helped me to my feet. I bent over the table and moaned with anticipation.

"Mmmm," I said, pushing my ass out towards him. He stroked my buttocks and I could hear him rubbing his cock.

"You're so hot," he said, "Fucking hell."

I purred and reached behind for his cock. He grabbed onto my hand and guided it back onto the table. He held both of my hands in front of me with his, then pushed his cock towards my pussy.

"You want to feel this inside you?" he whispered, "You want me to push my cock into you?"

"Yes!" I moaned desperately, "Yes, please. Please fuck me."

The postman pushed his cock slowly into my hot, wet vagina. I let out a contented moan as I finally felt what I'd been craving.

"Yes," I said as I bent over the table.

He spanked my ass again, then started to thrust into me. His thrusts were slow but powerful and I sensed that his tempo would gradually increase.

"Fuck me," I said, "Please, fuck me harder!"

I heard the postman's moans as he pushed his cock into me and squeezed my buttocks with his hands. He spanked me as his cock came out of me, then pushed himself deeply into me. I could feel the tip of his cock pushing against my G-spot as he fucked me deeply. I was moaning loudly with pleasure and my body was submissive across the table.

The postman's thrusts began to get faster, as I'd suspected they would. As his pace increased, the stimulation on my G-spot became more intense and I began to lose control. My leg involuntarily kicked the air as the pleasure got more and more powerful and my screams got louder.

"Yes!" I moaned, "Yes! Keep fucking me. Oh yes!"

"You filthy slut," he said as he fucked me. His hands were on my breasts and then my ass and then gripping onto my thighs. He picked up the belt again and hit me with the leather tip.

He leaned back as he fucked me, hitting me hard with the belt. As the pain mixed with the pleasure, it worked to intensify it. The stinging continued even as he put the belt down and pulled my body closer into his.

Suddenly, he reached around and grabbed onto my clitoris. His fingers stroked my clit firmly and quickly as he fucked me faster and faster. I lost control completely to his power and felt my vagina begin to clench. I gasped and screamed and gasped some more as I became faint with pleasure. My pussy spasmed on his hard cock and I felt a warm rush going through my body. My hands gripped the table as I collapsed into it, my muscles continuing to move involuntarily as I orgasmed hard.

He fucked me faster and faster and faster, then pulled his dick out of me and soaked my back in hot semen. I moaned as I revelled in his cum and felt his body pounding with orgasm. He kissed my neck and pushed his warm body against mine.

February 22st, 2001

After the meeting, Tom didn't need to wait for my invitation. He followed me to my car and got in to the passenger seat.

"That was so hot," he said as I drove towards my apartment, "Watching you squirming like that, watching you so obviously feeling that kind of pleasure in front of the whole room."

I turned to look at him briefly before focusing my eyes back on the road. God, he was so gorgeous. He was nearly 20 years younger than me, but we had a connection. He also had exceptional stamina and an extremely open mind.

"I just wanted to fuck you there and then," I said to him, "You do realise that, when we get back, you're getting eaten alive."

"Yes please," said Tom.

When we arrived at my apartment, I unlocked the door as quickly as possible. We walked inside and Tom immediately pushed me against the wall.

He took my breath away as he kissed me. There was passion, excitement and an element of playfulness about his kisses that made them addictive and extremely enjoyable. He bit the bottom of my lip, then licked the tip of my tongue with his. Our tongues entwined as he pushed his body into mine.

"I'm supposed to be fucking you," I managed to say, as I pushed him slightly away from me. He reached into his pocked and pulled out the remote-control to the vibrator. He laughed as he turned it up full, rendering me suddenly helpless against the wall.

"No," he said, "I'm fucking you."

It was never clear who was in control with us two. Indeed, it changed a lot. Still, he seemed determined to be the one in charge on this occasion.

Tom took my hand and led me to my bed. He pushed me down and pulled down my office trousers. I kicked off my heels as he did this and he took off his own shoes. The vibrator was still buzzing in my panties and I moaned with pleasure as the sensations hit me in waves. He spanked my pussy lightly, pushing the vibrator into me as he did.

He pulled down his trousers and boxers to reveal his huge erection. His cock was long and hard and I licked my lips as I saw it. He kissed me again.

As I unbuttoned his shirt, he undid my blouse. We became topless together, then I reached around and unhooked my bra. He pulled down my panties and put the vibrator to the side of me.

Tom buried his head into my crotch and his tongue teased my clit. He looked up at me, cheekily as he saw the obvious pleasure in my face. He licked me from side to side and grabbed on to my ass.

"Mmmm," he said into my soaking pussy, which became wetter as he licked me, "Mmmm you're so wet. You taste good."

I moaned and threw my head back as I felt his warm tongue against my clit. I ran my fingers through his dark hair.

Tom looked up at me, then kissed my thigh. He licked my torso and all the way up my breasts, nibbling at my nipple before licking up to my neck. I ran my fingers down his glistening back and reached down to his ass. I stroked his buttocks and reached around to stroke his balls. He gasped as I touched him there, then reached for his cock.

He guided it inside me, making us both inhale loudly with the releasing sensation.

"Oh God, Tom," I moaned as he started to fuck me. It was what I'd wanted all day.

"I've been waiting for this all day," he said.

I knew we had a connection.

"Me too," I replied enthusiastically, moving my hips to match his thrusts. We fucked each other rhythmically, staying in the same position for a long time. When I got close to coming, my hands gripped firmly onto his buttocks. He knew that this was a sign I was close to orgasm and he increased the speed of his thrusts. I stopped matching him and allowed him to fuck me whilst my orgasm took over me.

"Tom," I moaned, "Tom, oh my God,"

The orgasm took over and my body spasmed into his. My breath shallowed and I didn't stop moaning as his dick continued to fill my vagina.

"Turn around," he said as he pulled himself out of me.

I turned around and lifted my body up.

"I love fucking you doggy-style," he said excitedly as he pushed his cock into me again. At this angle, I could really feel it pushing at my G-spot and I gasped loudly. The pleasure was so much, I found myself screaming. I heard him groaning and moaning with pleasure and I reached around to grab at his firm, tight buttocks.

"Oh God," he said as I gripped his ass. I allowed my fingers to reach around close to his asshole.

"Oh, Layla!" He moaned as I touched the edge of his asshole. He fucked me quickly and with a lot of energy as I continued to gasp, moan and scream. He reached around and slapped my clitoris and I collapsed onto the bed. His body followed mine and he continued to fuck me. My hand was still on his ass, following the thrusts he controlled. I moved my hips again, increasing the speed of our fucking. Now I was in control. I ground against him whilst he pushed himself into me.

"It's so deep!" I moaned as his dick seemed to touch me in places I'd never been touched before.

I felt faint as we continued to fuck like this for much longer than I'd have deemed possible. When his dick got even harder than before, and we both knew he was going to come, Tom pulled himself out of me.

"Turn around," he instructed me again, which I did.

He came all over my face and chest with more spunk than I knew men were capable of releasing.

"You're so hot," he said again.

I pulled his face into mine and kissed him.

February 26st, 2001

I couldn't believe it when my boss invited me into his office. I knew I'd been naughty, viewing that stuff in work hours but my God – sometimes there was literally nothing to do. I wouldn't have watched it whilst I should have been working on something else.

I tried to hold on to some hope that it mightn't be that he wanted to talk about, but I couldn't genuinely convince myself. I knew that it was. He'd mentioned 'internet history' in the email, demanding that I go and see him, and I doubted he'd have a problem with anything else I'd searched for. I felt timid as I knocked on his door.

"Come on in, Layla," he said. I walked inside.

"Take a seat," he said. His face was straight and difficult to read. My heart was racing. I needed this job, to pay for my apartment and my *life*.

"I'm sorry," I began.

My boss – Mr Parker – he doesn't let even the highest up in the firm call him by his first name – continued to stare at me.

"Layla," he said, "Do you know why you're here?"

I stared at the floor. "I'm sorry, Mr Parker," I said.

"I didn't ask you if you were sorry," he said, raising his voice slightly, but not so much that it could be heard from outside the room. "I asked if you knew why you were here."

I took a deep breath.

"I think so," I said.

"Look at me," he said.

I looked up and stared at him. There was no use faking bravado, I knew I'd done wrong, and it looked as though I was going to pay for it.

"I want you to tell me what you've done," he said. He moved his chair out from his desk and sat directly opposite me, with his hands on his lap.

I looked at his crotch, by accident, then blushed and looked away. Mr Parker laughed.

"Layla," he said, "What have you done wrong?"

"I've..." I was struggling to say it. I'm not normally a shy person, but there's something about Mr Parker that makes me feel minute.

"Go on," he said, "Say it."

"I've been watching porn," I said quietly. My hands were shaking and I was struggling to breathe properly.

"And what does that make you?" Mr Parker asked calmly.

"It makes me badly behaved," I said, not knowing how else to respond.

"Yes, that," he said, "But what else does that make you?"

I said nothing, but shook my head slightly as I looked at him.

"It makes you a dirty little slut," he said.

I nodded, prompting him to smiled at me slightly.

"Lucky for you," he said, "I have a soft spot for little sluts."

Seeing and hearing Mr Parker like this, I couldn't help but start to get wet. I knew, deep down, that I shouldn't feel like I did, but I couldn't help it. There was something so effortlessly sexy about his total dominance and the was he was speaking to me. I knew he was degrading me. I knew he didn't one-hundred percent respect me, but I liked it.

I nodded at him.

"The porn you were watching," he said, "It was quite extreme, wasn't it?"

I felt myself flushing again. It had been extreme, as well. One particularly quiet afternoon, when there was practically nobody in the office, I'd watched some gang-bang porn. I'd used the remote-control vibrator that Tom had given to me and got myself off under the table. It brightened up what would have been a boring afternoon.

"Yes," I answered. Mr Parker stood up.

He walked towards me and unzipped his trousers. Immediately, his hard cock poked out through his fly-hole. He pointed his cock at me.

"I think you know what to do," he said.

I nodded and took his cock in my mouth. He stared down at me as I sucked him dutifully. After the first few sucks, I got more into it and became playful with my tongue. I licked him up and down, then sucked him hard. I took his cock to the back of my throat and bobbed my head back and forth furiously, hungrily. I'd never known how much I wanted Mr Parker's cock, until I had it in my mouth.

Suddenly, he pulled his cock out of my mouth and leaned over me. The leather office chair I was sat on bent backwards, so I was half-lying back. I spread my legs and welcomed his body between my thighs. He reached up my skirts and pulled down my tiny, black thong.

"This is very slutty underwear to wear to work," he said as he threw it on the floor, "But then, you are a dirty little slut, aren't you?"

"Mmmm," I nodded, staring at his cock as he pulled his trousers down. With his lower-half naked, he pushed his body into me again. I needed him to use it. I needed him to push it inside me.

Luckily, he felt the same kind of urgency. Mr Parker shoved his cock into my soaking pussy and started to thrust deeply into me.

"Dirty little slut on my office chair," he said as he fucked me aggressively. My hands gripped onto his back and I watched his face lose its usual level of composure. As the pleasure we both felt grew, my inhibitions completely ceased to exist and his faded a lot, too. I watched as his mouth opened with his moans as he fucked me from above. Pulling him closer, I felt his stubble on my cheek, scratching me and no doubt making my cheeks red as he fucked me faster and faster. I felt the sweat soaking his shirt as he succumbed to the pleasure, prioritising it above all else.

His fast, furious thrusts brought me close to orgasm quickly, as there was no time or space to think or feel anything but the intensely pleasurable sensations. I gasped and moaned loudly, which made him put his hand over my mouth. With his hand over my mouth, my breathing shallowed and pushed me over the edge. My body tensed and I felt my vaginal muscles contract on his hard, throbbing, also close-to-climaxing cock. I came fiercely with him inside me and grabbed onto his ass. I poked my fingers close to his asshole and his entire body jerked. He released himself inside me and gasped and collapsed onto me. I felt his heart pounding and his sweat covered my chest.

"I'm glad we have an understanding," he whispered to me breathlessly.

March 10st, 2001

I'd be lying if I said I wasn't up for fun last night. I was gagging for it, to be frank. But I didn't expect to have *that* much of a good time. It started in the hotel bar.

I sat alone, on a stool to the side of the bar. There was a gin and tonic in front of me and I was starting to feel good. The day had been reasonably stimulating, verging on rewarding and my self-esteem was in a good place. I sipped my drink through the straw, then twirled it around in the liquid. I felt eyes on me, but I didn't look up.

Before I left my hotel room, I'd treated myself to a luxurious shower. These trips always had the huge bonus of top grade hotels and rooms. I'd been asked to accompany the boss to an 'important' meeting. He'd hardly given me any details, but then, that was his style. He liked to use me as his personal assistant sometimes. I was always happy for the change. Even when I was married, I enjoyed a couple of these trips. The work was busy and varied and the evenings were long and free. I always had the evenings to myself, even in the early days.

After my shower, I'd put on a short, black dress. It's not the sort of thing I'd normally wear for a quiet evening in, but then, that wasn't what I wanted yesterday evening. I'd paired it with fishnet stockings, then put on my thigh-high, black boots. You could say that I looked like a slut.

Sitting to the side of the bar, sipping my gin, I knew that it was only a matter of time before I was approached. I just hoped that it was by somebody worthwhile.

Unable to ignore my curiosity any longer, I looked up in the direction I sensed the gaze coming from. Immediately, a man , stood at the bar, looked away. I considered his profile. From the back, he looked attractive. He was tall, quite slim and dressed sharply, in a suit. His stance suggested that he had confidence and his trousers showed off a nicely shaped ass. I nodded gently in approval, then looked again at my drink. I felt the look again. I picked up my book.

Half-reading a small book of poetry, I continued to feel the gaze. I knew that the man was looking at me. I was so curious to see what his face looked like. I looked up.

This time, the man didn't look away. His eyes met mine as he finished his pint. He smiled and put the glass down on the bar. Then, he started to walk towards me.

Staring at him directly, I noticed that I made him feel a little self-conscious as he walked closer. I also noticed that he was extremely handsome. This man – whose name I later found out was Mark – stunned me the second I saw his face. He had dark eyes to match his dark hair and a small, very well groomed dark beard. He looked slightly moody, but more mysterious, and his walk showed that he definitely, one-hundred percent had a lot of confidence. This made that moment of self-consciousness that I thought I spotted on his approach all the more special.

"I noticed your drink's empty," he said, nodding at my almost empty glass, "So's mine. Would you like another?"

I smiled at him with my mouth closed. I knew that, with the bright red lipstick I wore, my lips looked luscious and smiling at him like this would make him look at them.

I looked at my glass and swirled the straw around in it again. I lowered my face to it and sucked on the straw, still looking the man in the eye.

"I don't even know your name," I said, drawing my lips away from the straw.

"I'm Mark," he said, smiling at me knowingly and putting his hand in his pocket, "And I'm getting you a drink. You can tell me your name in a minute."

Mark walked towards the bar and ordered himself a pint and me another gin and tonic. That would have been my opportunity to walk away, had I not wanted his attention. I did want his attention, though. Very much so...

When Mark returned, he'd taken his jacket off and put it over his arm. He put mine and his drinks on the table, then his jacket on the back of the chair. His shirt was white, crisp and looked as though it had only been on an hour.

"So, what brings you here?" I asked. He smiled and shook his head.

"That would be telling," he said, then looked me up and down. "Maybe it's beautiful women like you," he said.

I raised my eyebrow at him. I liked him, I found him sexy, but lines like that just amused me. He seemed to recognise this, and laughed, himself.

"What about you?" He asked.

"I'm not telling if you aren't," I said, playing his game. I was having fun.

Mark nodded and sipped his pint. "What's the book?" He said, gesturing at the poetry book that was now lying on the table.

"Poetry," I said, "A collection of."

He nodded.

"I like poetry," he said, "Larkin's a favourite of mine. Are you keen?"

I felt delighted. I loved it when men liked poetry.

"Oh, yes," I said, "I do like Larkin. What I have here is a selection of Lawrence, and Hughes."

"Excellent," he said, "What's your favourite by Hughes?"

We talked for a while about poetry, as our drinks emptied. We were both genuinely enjoying the conversation and ended up buying another drink. It was during that one that the subject matter heated up a little.

"I like your stockings," he'd said, "I'd like to write a poem about taking them off."

The thought of him writing a poem about us having sex had turned me on so much, I touched myself there and then in the bar.

"I'd like to write a poem about your cock," I said, daringly. He looked at my hand as I touched myself and reached down to grab it. His hand stroked my soaking pussy as we sat in the hotel bar. Both of us looked around, but nobody was nearby.

"You're warm, wet and welcoming," he said, fingering my pussy. I writhed on his hand and moaned softly.

"I think we should go upstairs," he said after we shared a long kiss in the bar. I nodded in silent agreement and followed him up to his room...

Before we even got to his room, we couldn't keep our hands off each other. When we made it there, we were immediately on the bed. Mark pushed me so I lay with my legs open and his legs between them. His hard cock was pushing against my pussy before he even removed his trousers.

He unzipped my dress with urgency and I helped him to remove it. Then I partially unbuttoned his shirt before he pulled it over his head. He unbuttoned and pulled down his trousers as I took off my soaking thong. My boots were still on, but he grabbed on to them.

"Leave the boots on," he said as his naked body mounted mine. I wrapped my fishet-stockinged legs in thigh-high boots around his body and he immediately pushed his hard cock into me. I looked into his dark mysterious eyes as he settled quickly into a steady rhythm.

"Women like you just need to be fucked," he said to me as he pushed himself in and out of me. I moaned in agreement and grabbed his ass as he fucked me.

Our bodies established a mutual rhythm as we both gave and experienced an increasing amount of pleasure. I stared at his slightly hairy, slim chest and he pinched one of my nipples. Lowering his body further onto mine, Mark fucked me even faster. I grabbed onto his dark hair and gripped it as he grunted on top of me.

Animalistically, Mark grabbed onto my hair and fucked me fiercely. I screamed beneath him as he shoved his dick in and out of me, hitting my G spot and stimulating my clitoris simultaneously. Mark grabbed onto my boots and pushed my legs up either side of me. He stared down at me as he fucked me quickly and urgently and I felt the pleasure reaching the point of no return. I gasped as I looked up at him and felt myself bucking with pleasure. The tingling sensations I felt seemed to multiply and all become joined at the same time as I orgasmed powerfully with his cock still fucking me with passion.

Mark slapped my breasts as he started to fuck me even quicker.

"Women like you," he said, "Need to be fucked properly."

I nodded in agreement and thrust with him. I looked up into his dark eyes, which gave nothing away. He leaned down and kissed me, then kissed my neck. He started to bite me, making me moan even louder.

"Mark," I moaned, "Oh God,"

He bit me harder and spanked my ass as he fucked me. His dick was rock-hard inside me and I could tell he was going to come, soon.

He spanked me again and fucked me even faster. He reached down and pinched my nipple, then bit my neck again.

I was gasping as the sensations overwhelmed me.

I reached around to Mark's ass and squeezed his buttock. I spanked him and squeezed again. I poked my finger lightly into his asshole.

Mark gasped and yelped as his body seemed to tense. I watched his mouth open and heard him gasp again as I pushed my finger a little further into his ass. He moaned loudly and bucked as he came inside me. As he filled me with semen, his body relaxed on top of mine. I ran my fingers down his back and squeezed his skin as I felt him releasing his semen into my pussy. His hands found mine and our fingers entwined as we lay, spent, on the hotel bed.

March 24st, 2001

I was helpless. My hands and ankles were tied, my mouth was gagged and I was blindfolded. My perception of time was distorted, I had no control and I didn't know what he was going to do next. I was truly at his mercy.

"This is stage one of your punishment," he said. His voice sounded so deep, so serious. I tried to move but I couldn't. I wanted him to touch me, but he wouldn't. Not yet.

He said nothing else for a while, leaving me wondering what was going on. He liked to leave me wondering that.

After what felt like an eternity, I suddenly felt a sensation on my ass. It wasn't the sharp, painful sensation I'd been expecting, but a soft, tickling feeling. I felt my buttocks twitching.

The tickling sensation continued as the material stroked my ass. Suddenly, it stopped

Strike.

The pain began. I flinched at the first hit, which was quickly followed by another.

"This is still stage one," the voice said. I was powerless to respond.

There was another strike, and another, then silence again. The tickling returned, then suddenly stopped.

Silent and without contact for what felt like another eternity, I was accompanied by stinging sensations this time. I envisaged my red buttocks. My clitoris was throbbing. I tried to move, but couldn't.

I heard his footsteps around the room. I didn't know what was coming next, but I imagined that it would be 'stage two'. I waited.

The footsteps stopped and I sensed his presence close to me. Suddenly, I was screaming.

There was a tickling, tingling, impossible to describe sensation entirely dominating me. It took me several seconds before I recognised it as the pin-wheel. I giggled and squealed as it went across my bare buttocks and around my vulva. I heard him laughing.

"That wasn't stage two," he said, "That was just for my own amusement."

The sensation stopped. I gasped for breath and felt saliva escaping my mouth due to the gag.

Suddenly, I felt a strong strike.

"This is stage two," he said.

The heavy, thudding strike took me by surprise, though of course it shouldn't have. The sharp, stinging sensation was familiar though somehow I always forgot its intensity. He struck me again and I started to drift into a different state of mind.

As the spanking with the studded paddle continued, the pain got harder and harder to bear. I was aware that my mouth was soaked as I lost control of my tongue and I knew my pussy was wet, too. As suddenly as it had began, the spanking stopped.

I felt his firm hand stroking my buttocks.

"I'm trying to decide," he said, "Whether you've been naughty enough for stage three."

I, of course, couldn't respond. Nor was I supposed to. I waited patiently for him to decide.

"Yes," he said eventually, "Yes, you have."

To my surprise, he untied my wrists and ankles, then removed my gag and blindfold. I looked into his blue eyes, questioning what he had in mind. I looked adoringly at his composed stance. He was fully clothed in a black shirt, black trousers and boots and he hooked one of his fingers into his pocket. He smiled at me sadistically.

"What's stage three?" I whispered. He looked amused, which somehow added to his powerfulness.

"Stage three," he said, "Requires your going home, right now."

I couldn't help but protest. I needed him. I needed him for longer than this.

"No," I started, "Please, please, Sir."

He shook his head firmly.

"I'll see you tomorrow," he said, "Maybe."

His eyes glistened as he watched me accept the reality.

"Naughty girls," he said, "Need to be punished."

He kissed me on the forehead then gestured at my clothes, which lay on the floor. He watched me as I dressed myself, then nodded at the door.

"Goodbye, Layla," he said, "You will learn to be good."

"Goodbye, Sir," I whispered. I walked out of the dungeon, under his gaze.

March 28st, 2001

"Please," I begged him, shamelessly, as he stood before me with his cock exposed. He looked at my naked body.

"You need to learn patience," he said as he tied my ankles together. He did the same with my wrists, then stood over me. He had a large vibrator in his hand, which wasn't yet switched on.

I stayed silent for several seconds before involuntarily groaning. I was desperate for his cock and he knew it. He'd been teasing me for days and it was becoming unbearable.

He twisted the vibrator on to a low speed, then approached my clitoris with it.

I moaned loudly as it began to stimulate me. I stared lovingly into his eyes and thanked him.

"Thank you," I said, staring at his cock. I reached my tongue out, to tell him I wanted to lick his cock, but he already knew.

Leaving the vibrator placed between my legs, stimulating me lightly, he approached my mouth with his cock. He pushed it towards my begging mouth and I let it all in. I sucked it gently, the way I knew he liked it, as I enjoyed hearing his groans of pleasure. He let me suck him for several minutes, before pulling his cock away from me. He picked up the vibrator and turned it up a little more.

"I bet you're dying to come, aren't you?" He said, half-laughing. I nodded, watching his muscular arm as he guided the vibrator back to my clitoris. He turned it up to almost full speed as I writhed uncontrollably beneath it. I squealed as he rubbed it quickly from side to side, before pushing it into my soaking vagina. He fucked me with the vibrator, then pulled it away and spread my legs apart.

"I'm going to fuck you so hard," he said, "You're going to be glad you waited for this."

I instinctively tried to reach out to him but my hands were tied. He gripped my arms and pushed his cock into me as his lips met mine. He kissed me passionately as we both moaned with pleasure at the release we'd been waiting for. He thrust into me meaningfully and slowly whilst he continued to kiss me. When we stopped kissing, he reached behind me to pick something up.

As he tightened nipple clamps onto me, his dick continued to push in and out of my warm, wet vagina. The pain of the clamps made me focus on the pleasure. The pleasure of his cock in me.

"This," he whispered, "Is what happens when you're a good girl."

The sound of his voice calling me a "good girl" made me feel as though I was going to melt. My heart fluttered as the tingles of pleasure spread and I felt my face smiling with pleasure. I looked up and saw that his was, too.

"Good girl," he said again, before thrusting into me suddenly more deeply. He quickened his pace and fucked me hard as I was powerless beneath him.

"Yes," I moaned, "Oh, yes. This is so good. Thank you, Sir."

He tightened the clamps even more as he fucked me, then pushed down on my pelvis with his hand. The combined sensations left me even more powerless as I gave in to the sensations and lost control of my body. I felt warm liquid releasing from my vagina as I squirted all over his hard dick and I heard myself screaming with pleasure as though the sound was coming from somebody else's mouth.

He moaned loudly as his dick got even harder inside me. He thrust harder and harder and I saw the familiar distortion of his face.

"Layla," he gasped as he released his semen inside me. "Layla," he said again, breathlessly as his orgasm began to fade. "Layla," he said again, before he kissed me on the forehead.

April 7st, 2001

I'd be lying if I said I wasn't nervous when I walked into Daz and Sheila's house the night before last. It's taken me so long to write about it because I've only just got over it all!

Well, we did the thing. The thing we've talked about for weeks, months, even. I don't think any of us thought that it would ever actually happen. It happened.

I got there at 7.32pm, exactly. I know that because I actually arrived at their house a bit before 7.30 – the arranged time – but I didn't want to appear too keen. Two minutes late seemed appropriately 'on time' whilst still not overly eager. Sheila opened the door.

She was dressed in black underwear with a translucent black nightgown over her. She looked a little nervous, too, but she had a large glass of red wine in her hand. Just looking at it made me feel a little calmer.

"Come in," she said, smiling. I followed her inside. Music was playing and the room smelt like patchouli and vanilla. When we walked into the living room, Daz sat on the sofa. He was smiling and also had a glass of wine. As soon as he saw me, he stood up.

"Layla," he said, looking me up and down. I wore a red dress, as the couple had requested the last time we spoke about this. I also wore hold-up black stockings and bright red, high heeled shoes. My lipstick matched.

"Would you like a glass of wine?" He said, "Red, perhaps?"

I laughed and walked towards him. He kissed me on the cheek, then squeezed my ass before walking to the kitchen. Sheila smiled at me.

"You look great," she said, "Really sexy in that red."

I smiled at her. It was the first time I'd seen her in her underwear and she looked great, too. I stared at her breasts.

"You look amazing, Sheila," I said, sincerely. "Your breasts look so good. I had no idea they were that big."

Sheila laughed and stroked the front of her nipples, which I could tell were erect. She walked towards me and leaned in for a kiss. Our lips met, then our tongues entwined playfully. I felt her breasts against mine as we embraced and kissed gently. Daz returned to the room.

"Great to see you getting along so well," he said, deeply, as he passed me the glass of wine. I smiled at Daz. I'd always liked him. He was an attractive man who worked hard to supply for his family. His hair was greying but he'd kept a youthful face and he never had facial hair. He was dressed casually, in jeans and a white t-shirt. The short sleeves showed off tattoos on his arms that I hadn't known he had. Sheila was attractive, too. She had long, brown hair, was quite thin but had large breasts, I'd just realised. Daz and Sheila had been married for 15 years and their relationship was healthy and strong. They'd mentioned having threesomes before, but I knew it wasn't something they did regularly.

"Thank you," I said, accepting the glass and immediately taking a large sip. "Cheers," I said, "Here's to a great evening!"

"To a great evening," Sheila said, looking at me suggestively. She was so horny, I could tell. Her pupils were dilated, her voice had taken a slightly husky turn and was staring at me like she couldn't wait to get started. Her eagerness relaxed me.

Daz sat down on their large, leather sofa and patted the space next to him. I looked at Sheila, who nodded at me.

"Sit down," she said. I went and sat right next to Daz.

Sheila immediately came and sat next to us – next to me – and put her hand on my leg.

"You look so good in red," she said, stroking my stockinged thigh.

"Thanks," I said, turning to her and smiling. "And you look gorgeous. I can't get over how big your breasts are."

I stared at her breasts again. She smiled and opened the nightgown she wore fully.

"Touch them," she said. I reached out and stroked her smooth, silky skin. I allowed my hand to brush across her erect nipples simultaneously and watched her shiver with delight.

She opened her mouth slightly and, before I knew it, our mouths were together. Her soft, gentle lips seemed to caress mine as we shared a long, increasingly passionate kiss. I felt Daz's hand on my right thigh, reaching up towards my red thong. I was soaking and my clit was throbbing. I reached behind me and immediately found his hard cock in his jeans. I stroked it as I continued to kiss Sheila.

Sheila moaned and wrapped her leg around mine. She pushed her pelvis towards me and I knew that she wanted to be touched. I slid my hand down and into her black panties. She immediately gasped as I stroked her clitoris. She was shaven and her skin was smooth and warm. I hooked my finger around to touch the entrance to her vagina, moaning myself as I felt how wet she was. I felt a hand stroking my own pussy.

Without thinking about what I was doing, I lowered my head to Sheila's crotch. I licked her thighs and quickly approached her clitoris with my tongue. I licked her slowly and gently as the lower half of my own body landed on top of Daz. He spanked my ass as I licked his wife, then slid his body out from beneath me. Within seconds, I felt his hard cock poking at my ass, as I continued to lick his increasingly aroused wife.

Sheila wrapped her legs around my head and moaned loudly with pleasure. Daz playfully circled my vulva with his cock. I tried to push myself into him, but he was in charge. He spanked me again, then slapped his cock against my ass.

I licked Sheila even more quickly, then stuck my tongue into her vagina. She gasped loudly at the unexpected move, then I reached around and grabbed her ass. I buried my face into her vulva, sucking on her clitoris then licking her widely from side to side, moaning with arousal and anticipation as I pleasured her.

Suddenly, Daz pushed his cock into me. I screamed with pleasure before licking Sheila's clitoris furiously. She screamed to as her legs tightened around my head whilst she got closer to orgasm.

Daz fucked me quickly from behind and I gasped into Sheila's pussy. She gripped onto my hair and pulled it slightly, whilst pushing herself firmly into my face. I felt her stomach buck as her clitoris seemed to explode in my mouth. It went from throbbing, firmly and with extreme excitement to pulsating powerfully in a consistent rhythm. I looked up and saw clearly that Sheila was orgasming. Her face was fixed in an ecstatic release and her chest was pounding, moving her breasts with each heart beat.

I pulled my face away from her pussy and got up onto my hands and knees as Daz continued to fuck me. I stared at her breasts and felt myself about to come with Daz's powerful thrusts. I grabbed Sheila's breast and allowed myself to feel the release. Tingles seemed to spread across my pelvis and it was as though fireworks went off inside my body. Daz released himself from me whilst I was still orgasming and I collapsed on the sofa momentarily. He walked over to Sheila and kissed her passionately, then immediately entered her.

As he fucked Sheila with equal vigour, he reached across and stroked my clit again. Sheila turned and licked my breasts as she was fucked by Daz.

"On your hands and knees, Sheila," Daz said to her, "You know what to do."

Sheila smiled and looked at me naughtily. She got onto her hands and knees beside me and pulled me so that I had my pussy in her face. She started to lick my tender, sensitive post-orgasm pussy and I immediately screamed with pleasure. Daz entered her from behind, gripping onto her hair.

As Sheila licked me, with a growing amount of pressure and pace, Daz fucked her energetically. She moaned into my pussy and I felt her gasps sucking at my own warm, wet genitals. When she came, Sheila licked me even faster. She seemed to lose herself in my vagina as she screamed into it and gasped as her body shook.

Daz also sped up amazingly and exhaled loudly as he filled Sheila with come. She continued to lick me until I orgasmed powerfully on her face. My legs hooked around her neck as Daz partially collapsed onto the two of us.

Sheila kissed her way up my body, then our mouths met again.

To be continued...

CPSIA information can be obtained
at www.ICGtesting.com
Printed in the USA
FSHW011258020819
60657FS